A IS FOR AARRGH!

ALSO BY WILLIAM J. BROOKE

A Telling of the Tales: *Five Stories*

Untold Tales

A Brush with Magic

Teller of Tales

WILLIAM J. BROOKE

A IS FOR AARRGH!

JOANNA COTLER BOOKS
An Imprint of HarperCollins*Publishers*

A Is for Aarrgh!
Copyright © 1999 by William J. Brooke

Library of Congress Cataloging-in-Publication Data
Brooke, William J.
   A is for aarrgh! / William J. Brooke.
      p.   cm.
   "Joanna Cotler books."
   Summary: Mog, a young boy living during the Stone Age, discovers words and language
and teaches his fellow cave dwellers how to talk, thus altering the course of history.
   ISBN 0-06-023393-1. — ISBN 0-06-023394-X (lib. bdg.)
   [1. Language and languages—Fiction.   2. Communication—Fiction.   3. Prehistoric
peoples—Fiction.]   I. Title.
PZ7.B78977Ig   1999   99-14827
[Fic]—dc21   CIP

Typography by Alicia Mikles
1   2   3   4   5   6   7   8   9   10
❖
First Edition

For Karen

my friend and colleague

my Mabel, my Yum-Yum

and, above all, my Elsie

who gave life to my Point

And for Lynne

who gives point to my life

I

"AARRGH!" (POINT)
[SUN]

Brog swung his club fiercely and missed by only about ninety-three million miles.

The others didn't know he'd missed the big yellow thing in the sky by so much, but they wouldn't have commented even if they did. Brog was much stronger than any of them, and his reach, while not in the ninety-three-million-mile class, was more than enough to rattle their brains.

So their shouts were all approval and encouragement.

"Well done!" yelled Pog. She was married to Brog and believed in being encouraging.

"Good shot!" shouted Shog, who always tried to agree. In a time when everyone carried clubs, this was not a bad policy.

"Yes, well done!" echoed Drog, baring his teeth in

I

a big smile. Then, with a quick glance to be sure no one could hear him, he muttered through those same teeth, "You big blowhard."

"My toe hurts where I stubbed it yesterday!" yelled Quog. This had nothing to do with what was going on, but it was what Quog was thinking about at the moment, so it was what he said. He could never really believe that anything in the world was more important than his personal well-being.

"You almost got it that time!" Pog continued. That wasn't strictly true, but she was very proud of her husband and didn't mind stretching a point to encourage him. "It's trying to ignore you, but that one got its attention."

Then they all waited to see if the mighty swing of the club had accomplished its purpose. It hadn't.

The big yellow thing in the sky ignored them completely. Well, maybe it hesitated a moment (it really had been a good swing, and the club was especially big and gnarly), but then it pressed on toward the bank of white, puffy things.

Brog was not the type to give up. He gave an earsplitting howl. He displayed his ferocious, snarly teeth. He jumped up and down and waved his arms.

He did a back flip (which could have been dangerous, but fortunately he landed on his head).

Pog joined in and then everyone else, backing him up in a gibbering chorus of shrieks and groans and chest-thumpings. Anybody with any sense would have been terrified, but heavenly bodies are obliviously self-centered. The big yellow thing showed no sign of being intimidated. Calmly and without hurry, it slid behind the big fluffy things and out of sight.

Which is to say, the sun went behind a cloud. Not just *a* cloud, a whole sky full of cloud. The bright glow of sunrise disappeared, and the world faded into shades of leaden gray.

Brog continued to dance in rage and wave his club. He knew it was useless, but he never let mere facts influence his actions. He was strong and brave and not particularly bright, a combination that has changed the course of human events on more than one occasion. He continued to leap and cavort at the very edge of the High Cliff, the highest spot in the Tribe's territory, leaning far out to get closer to his enemy. (Well, not really *enemy*. When the big yellow thing did its job properly—slid slowly up the sky and made everything nice and warm—it was regarded as a good friend.

Brog would have given it a friendly punch in the arm if he could have reached that far and found an arm to punch. But the big yellow thing was often lazy, preferring to sleep the day away behind the puffy things. At least that's what the Tribe assumed it did, since that's what they would have done, given the chance.)

As long as Brog kept up his display, so did the whole Tribe. It was something like an exercise class, but with lots more hair and no showers afterward. No one wanted Brog to think they hadn't done their best for him. Finally, Pog tapped him and said, "Brog, it's all right, that's enough. We'll just have to hope the sun rises again tomorrow and decides to stay awake."

Now, a couple of things before we go any further. First, it may seem odd that there was doubt about the sun rising, but this was happening very long ago, even before "once upon a time." Scientists had not yet discovered much of anything, including themselves, so there was no one to say, "The sun always rises" or "E equals MC squared" or "If it tastes good, it's bad for you."

No, everyone could only go by what they saw. Sometimes the sun rose in a businesslike fashion and efficiently carried out its tasks of warming and drying and being pleasant, eventually turning red (perhaps from all the effort) and yielding to the moon or stars or whoever else might wander across the sky. At other times, the sun would send out clouds and rain and thunder and lightning, and there was no point in leaving your cave unless you particularly liked being cold and wet and electrocuted.

Did I mention before that the Tribe lived in caves? They were, in fact, what we call "cavemen." Of course, they didn't call them*selves* cavemen. *Everyone* lived in caves, so that would just be repeating the obvious. We don't call ourselves "housepeople" or "apartmentpersons," and they didn't call themselves "cavemen."

So they were on the cliff outside their caves, and Pog tapped Brog and said, "Let's hope the sun rises tomorrow."

Well, no, that's another thing. She didn't say "the sun" because they didn't have names for anything yet, including the sun. It was "the big yellow thing that rose in the sky" and . . .

Well, actually, they didn't have *any* words yet. No "big yellow thing," no "sky," no "no," no "nothing." So what Pog really said was sort of "grunt, grunt,

grunt," with a finger pointed up to make her meaning crystal clear. Of course, she would have done the same thing to mean sky or bird or sixty-percent chance of precipitation, but she was picturing the big yellow thing in her mind while she grunted and pointed, so it seemed obvious to her.

Okay, that's all clear, which brings us up to where she said "Brog," and took his arm and—

Of course, if something as important as the sun didn't have a name, then Brog didn't either, even if he *was* the best hunter in those parts. What Pog did was look right at him and give him a tap, which meant "Hey, you" in the caveman style of communication. And it would have meant "Brog" if they had known that would turn out to be his name in Chapter 5.

Now, you might think a couple of grunts and a look are a feeble way to get your attention, and you'd be right. But you're forgetting the part about the tapping. This was the really impressive part of caveman communication, because the tapping was done with a large, gnarly and particularly hard wooden club, just like the one Brog had used to get the sun's attention.

Conversation was not a high priority for cavemen. If you pointed and grunted, that might mean

"I'm going over there." And if you bugged out your eyes and screamed real loud that probably meant "A woolly bison is about to trample me, and I'd appreciate some assistance if you're not too busy, thanks very much."

Around the caves, the only need for communication was if someone had something you wanted, like a nice haunch of meat. Then you'd tap him with your club to indicate direct address and point and grunt and maybe drool a bit to make it absolutely clear. If he didn't get the message, you'd repeat the process: tap, point, grunt, drool. And so on, each tap being a little more emphatic, with the first one being none too timid itself. Eventually, you would bring him to a state of either understanding or unconsciousness.

The translation of most conversations would have been something like this: "Give me that." "What? Ouch." "Give me that." "What? Ouch." "Give me that." "What? . . ." And so on. The best conversationalists were the ones with the fewest lumps on their heads. Brog wasn't very bright, but the only bumps on him were sweet nothings from his loving wife, Pog.

So if I told you this story the way Pog or Brog would tell it, it would go something like this:

Urggh!

Aarrgh!

(Point up.)

Rrrngh!

Nnnurgh!

(Shrug.)

Mrargh!

Gggrung!

I'll stop there before I give away the ending.

(Of course, I'm leaving out all the business with the club. You would pay much more attention to all that grunting if I could just reach out and give you a little tap with . . . But I'm joking. I would never think of bonking a faithful reader. So long as you remain attentive.)

Obviously, grunting doesn't make for a very exciting story. And if you try to read it out loud, it'll wear out your throat even faster than it wears out the "g" and the "r" on my keyboard. And since words were just about to be invented (that's what this story will be about if I can just get it started properly), I don't think it's unfair to bend the laws of time and space ever so slightly and let my characters speak for themselves.

Now, where were we?

Brog had swung his club at the sun, which was just the polite caveman way of getting its attention so he could express the Tribe's belief that it should stay out and do its job rather than slinking away behind the clouds. And now we're up to where Pog says, "It's all right, Brog." (I'm translating now, you remember). "We'll just have to hope the sun rises tomorrow. Come on back to the cave."

Brog let her lead him back toward their cave. The day was dark and dank, and it would be a relief to get in out of it. Of course, the cave was also dark and dank, but it was the place they called home ("grarrg," actually), and so that was where they would go.

Brog heard laughter behind him and turned to see what was happening.

Laughter, I should point out, existed even though words didn't. You couldn't discuss why the chicken crossed the road, but you could still get a good giggle out of someone falling in the mud. (Someone else, that is. The things that make you laugh when they happen to someone else are never funny when they happen to you.)

So Brog turned to see who was laughing and at what, and it had better not be at him. Out on the lip of the precipice, where Brog had just been performing, a tiny little boy was standing on his tiptoes and was making funny little smacking mouth noises as he waved his hands in the air.

Brog sighed. (There was a lot of sighing back then, too, maybe even more than laughing.) He threw a scowl at the laughers, who instantly stopped and slipped out of his reach and back to their caves.

The little boy was Mog, or soon would be. He was Brog's son, and his smallness was embarrassing. Since Brog was a very good hunter, he naturally believed that hunting skill was the most important talent a person could possess. He wanted his son to be a great hunter, but the boy was small and timid and Brog feared that he would never be good at anything, much less the hunt.

Brog listened to the silly noises coming from his son's mouth. Not a good, hearty "rrgg" combination in the lot. He wished he could have a good father-son talk, but the boy was so small that a little tap hello would have knocked him into the next county. (Do I need to mention there was no such thing as a county at this . . . no, of course, you knew that. Forget I interrupted.)

Mog looked up at Brog and smiled and said, "Papa."

This was another source of embarrassment to Brog, for this was not a translation. Mog didn't swing a club and growl fondly. He actually said "Papa." He went around all the time making mouth noises, and no one knew why. It was very rude just to start popping your lips at someone without even clubbing them hello. It certainly wasn't the sort of thing the son of a great hunter should be doing. When you were face-to-face with a cave bear, mouth noises were not going to help you.

Everyone said that Mog was a little "touched in the head." Specifically, they'd point at him and club themselves on the head. This needed no translation.

"Mama," said Mog to Pog as she joined the family group at the edge of the High Cliff. She secretly thought this was cute ("Grarrnh!" as she would put it), but knew it embarrassed Brog in front of the neighbors. So she hugged Mog close to hush him and carried him easily back to the cave.

Brog was too depressed to spend the day in the cave. He decided killing something might raise his spirits. Normally, there'd be no hunt on such a gloomy day, but if Brog was in the mood, the others didn't have much choice.

II

So Brog beat his chest and did some gibbering to call out the other inhabitants of Here (which was as close as this group of caves had to a name: you pointed down at the ground and that was Here; when you were somewhere else, you hooked your thumb over your shoulder and then Here was Back There). Then he brandished his club and pointed down toward the plains where the herds roamed.

There were some groans of "Do we have to?" which might have angered Brog, but the looseness of caveman speech allowed him to interpret it as "Okay, boss, let's go get 'em!" The others gathered the sharpened sticks that were their spears, and soon Brog was leading his little band of fierce hunters down the slope. "There will be feasting tonight!" he exclaimed, swinging the club, which was always his preferred weapon.

"I don't know why, but here we go!" shouted Shog, agreeably.

"Brog is a jerk," cheered Drog.

"I got a splinter!" yelled Quog, dropping his spear. It landed on his already stubbed toe. "Now my foot hurts even worse!" he shrieked.

Heartened by all the enthusiasm, Brog led them

down the slope. A good hunt was just the thing to forget his embarrassment over his son.

He didn't know that Mog and his silly noises would soon change the hunt forever.

Not to mention everything else.

2

"AARRGH!" (BONK)
[HUNT]

Ah, the thrill of the hunt! The fierce efficiency and deadly cunning of Man, the Predator!

In the ominous stillness, Brog gestured their directions: half that way and half this, hide behind the rocks, await my signal. They vanished into the tall grass, lurking silently, until Brog, prompted by his razor-sharp instinct, leaped out with a savage snarl. The herd of antelope froze in stunned shock, then bounded away, straight onto the spears that appeared from nowhere. With icy precision, the hunters acted as one. Nothing could stand against them. They carried the hapless beasts back to the caves, where the women made the feast and sang their songs of admiration for the bravery, strength and cleverness of this tight-knit band, this happy few. After the feast, the women overcame the men's natural modesty to make them reenact the great hunt. Tall shadows capered on rocky walls, and sparks flew up to the moon as the women sighed in envy and wonder at their mighty men and the thrill of the hunt.

Well . . .

No, they didn't.

Not any of it.

Brog could picture it in his mind, just that way, as he stared down at the antelope in the little valley. But it hadn't happened yet, ever, not like that. Not even close to it.

Brog wasn't sure why. The picture was so clear in his mind, why couldn't the others ever see what he was seeing?

Brog held up a hand for silence. Quog started to mention he had a stomachache, but Brog's club politely interrupted and shifted his attention to a splitting headache which hadn't been there a moment earlier. Before Drog could finish muttering "What a dope," he was stretched out beside Quog with a matching lump on his head. Shog was going to compliment Brog's backhand, but found himself staring up at the sky. Brog eyed Crog. He didn't say anything, so Brog clubbed him, too, just to be on the safe side.

Now that he had their attention, Brog gave his instructions. "Aarrgh," he whispered, pointing to each man and then a rock. "Aarrgh," he whispered, showing how they should hide. Then, "Aarrgh," he whispered, jumping out to strike with club or spear.

They all nodded to indicate their perfect understanding of this plan. Brog watched them disappearing into the tall grass. "Maybe they really did understand me, and we'll have our first really successful hunt," Brog thought. "Or maybe the antelope will all die of fright when I jump out." That seemed much more likely.

Brog peered over his rock at the dozen antelope browsing in the little clearing below. Enough time had passed for everyone to get in place, but he waited a bit longer. It was important that the animals be completely encircled and that they all strike at once so none could escape.

At that moment, Shog leaped up shouting from behind a rock a few yards away. Brog was annoyed but not surprised. If everyone was in place, the plan could still work. He leaped up himself, with a ferocious snarl. The antelope froze a moment, then bounded away.

Amazingly, all the other hunters were ready and

leaped out at just the same moment, brandishing their spears. It was really unusually good for them and Brog would have been very pleased, if only they hadn't all hidden together behind the same rock. They had gotten the part about hiding behind a rock, but the idea of encirclement had been too much for them. They stood scratching their heads and anything else they could conveniently reach, while Brog ran swiftly but hopelessly after the disappearing antelope.

Suddenly, Drog jumped up from behind a rock ahead of the antelope, startling one of them and turning it back toward Brog. A quick swing of his club brought that one down as the rest made their escape.

The other hunters wandered over to gaze with delight and surprise at the slain antelope. Then they shouted out their congratulations. To Drog. They all knew he was lazy and greedy and malicious, but somehow he had managed to be in just the right place at the right time and that made him the hero of the day.

Brog was quiet. He didn't want to point out that the idea of encirclement had been *his*. Moreover, *he* was the one who'd killed the antelope; Drog had just jumped up. But Drog *had* jumped up at just the right time, so Brog couldn't say anything against him.

So they brought the antelope home, and the women were disappointed there wasn't more, but glad there wasn't less. The women prepared the meat, and the men were all irritated that their portions weren't larger. (They always managed to forget that the women were only responsible for how the food was cooked, not how much there was.) The men were slow to yield to the women's urgings to reenact the hunt; it took almost ten whole seconds. (The women were actually interested only in the results of the hunt, not the details, but they knew the men needed to do a bit of strutting, so they kept up the pretense.)

The men leaped and capered and admired their shadows on the walls of rock, and the women stifled yawns and pasted on smiles of encouragement.

And Drog experienced the heady excitement of leading the action. He had never before done anything to impress the women, but now they were so taken with him they could barely conceal their gasps of admiration (or was it boredom?).

The one thing that Drog was good at was seeing which way the wind blew before deciding on a course of action. Which was why he was usually the last to do anything, particularly if it involved work or danger.

Which was why he had crawled off to that rock for a nap where the other hunters and their silly plans wouldn't bother him. Which was why he just happened to be in the path of the fleeing antelope. Which was why he jumped up in fear when his sleep was disturbed. Which was why he was acclaimed the hero of the day. And which was why he did nothing to correct their misunderstanding of his actions.

It was the first time Drog had ever been the center of attention.

It felt good. He wanted more of it. He thought about working harder on the next hunt, changing his whole life so he would deserve the admiration of the Tribe.

Then he laughed and got serious. It had to be possible to keep the attention without doing the work. He would think. He would watch his chance.

He would find a way.

3

"AARRGH!" (POINT)
[SUN AGAIN]

"Wake up, Brog," said Pog (I'm translating now, you remember). "It's time to see if the big yellow thing rises again."

Brog slowly crawled out from beneath the furs (with many grunts that I won't translate because their meaning was not at all nice). He had tossed and turned all night because thoughts had been racing through his head, faster than antelope and even more difficult for the great hunter to catch. Drog was there, creeping through the undergrowth of his mind and jumping up to startle him each time he caught up to the antelope of sleep.

"I'll wake Mog while you go wake the big yellow thing," Pog said, giving Brog a love tap that almost put him back to sleep.

Brog grumbled, but he never shirked his duty.

Stretching and yawning, he crawled out of the cave into the murky grayness of morning. There was mist and moisture. Just the sort of day the sun liked to sleep late. Brog understood its feelings all too well, but why should the big yellow thing get to take it easy when *he* didn't?

He moved up the slope of rock that was the Tribe's front yard to the High Cliff. The others gathered around him, scratching and yawning and looking like they needed that first cup of coffee that they wouldn't get for several thousand more years.

The mists filled the valleys below them, and there were some clouds in the sky, but it wasn't completely overcast. There was hope for the day. If Brog did his job properly.

He took the high point and swung his club a time or two just to limber up. He cleared his throat and practiced his "ggrr" sounds. It's not easy to get started in the morning, and there's nothing more embarrassing than a growl that cracks.

The first glimmer of dawn appeared, just a sliver of gold at the horizon. Brog sighted over his club to get the distance, then reared back and took a mighty swing.

He missed.

The sun was unimpressed. Gibber, jump, growl, shout, pound—it was pretty much a replay of yesterday's performance. The sun peeked out, then found a nest of clouds and was ready to settle in for the long run.

Everyone headed back to pass a day in the dim twilight of their caves. They were stopped by a sound behind them. Tiny little Mog had slipped away from Pog and crawled again onto the high rock. Before Pog could stop him, he raised himself to his full shortness and waved his hand at the sky in a little parody of his father's mighty swing. "Sun!" he called (and I'm not translating now). "Sun!"

Brog lowered his head in shame. Since he was only semi-erect to begin with, this pretty much put his lower lip in the dust.

"Sun!" repeated Mog.

Everyone watched with uncertainty. Their first impulse was to laugh out loud at Mog and his silly mouth noises. But Brog was still big and strong, and you didn't want to laugh at anyone in his family too openly. So everyone was very attentive just at that moment when . . .

The sun burst through the clouds and shone

brightly. The mists and the high puffs all began to burn away. The big yellow thing quickly became too bright to look at and beamed down upon an absolutely glorious day.

Mog lowered his hands and turned to smile at everyone. "Sun," he said happily.

No one knew quite what had happened. Had the mouth noise gotten the big yellow thing's attention, like hitting it with a club? Was it so annoyed by the sound that it came out of hiding? But if it wasn't annoyed by clubs, why would it mind a sound? Maybe it *liked* the sound. "Sun." It was a stupid sound, but there it was.

Now, *we* know of course that the sun's emergence had nothing to do with Mog's pronouncement. Any good weatherman could tell you that it was just the sudden arrival of a high pressure area behind a warm front, which created an inversion in the upper atmosphere, resulting in lower isobars of, um, that is higher, um, barometric . . . Well, any good weatherman could tell you what caused it, and like every good citizen you would turn off the TV and carry an umbrella because you don't trust any of that gibberish. I mean, why are they called meteorologists if they're supposed to know about the weather? Not that I'd trust them if they said a meteor was about to fall, either, but at least . . .

Well, never mind all that now. My point is that we now know what causes changes in the weather, unlike the poor, ignorant people of the Tribe. They could only watch and try to guess how Mog had succeeded when Brog had failed. Of course, it wasn't really cause and effect but simple coincidence that had made the sun come out at just the right moment.

Now, you may say it's not fair that coincidence should motivate such an important moment (which this certainly was, as we will soon see) and maybe you'd be right. But coincidence drives a depressing amount of what's really important in our lives. I know for a fact that a little boy about ten hillsides away had tried the same thing, pointing at the sun and calling out "Gorflimalblastic!" which was his name for the sun. Just at that moment . . . the volcano erupted. The people of that tribe didn't like the word any better than the volcano did, so they tossed the little boy into the closest crater and that was the end of that. So, you see, all Mog or any of us can really do is muddle on and hope the accidents fall more in our favor than against us.

Coincidence or not, the Tribespeople watched in amazement, and they would have been happy to sit around discussing it until they all had minor concussions, but Brog knew they should get on with the hunt while the weather was still nice. The big yellow thing was entirely capable of changing its mind, whether it had been lured out by clubs or mouth noises. Brog hurried the men along with taps of encouragement. They set off down the slope, brandishing their weapons and shouting out the mighty deeds they were going to perform that day while the women cheered them on with the cave equivalent of "Sure, honey, I don't doubt it for a minute, but I won't hold my breath."

For most of the men, this was the best part of the hunt: no one had done anything stupid yet, Brog hadn't thumped anyone too much, and the walk was downhill. So they set out briskly and happily, but they stopped in surprise when Mog took a place alongside Brog.

There came a time when all manchildren joined the hunt and began to learn, but Mog was the least likely of apprentices. Still, he *had* done something surprising that morning (just what, they weren't sure), so maybe he'd surprise them again.

Brog was embarrassed. Mog didn't even bring the little spear Brog had tried to teach him with. Brog was half pleased by what Mog had done that morning and half annoyed that Mog had succeeded (if, in fact, he had) where Brog had failed (if, in fact, he had). Oh, well, when it came to children, you were stuck with what you got.

So Brog made the best of it. He led them down into the grasslands, trying to ignore the giggles from his gallant little band at Mog's continuous mouth noises. When they came upon some antelope, Brog gave his usual performance of the Sonata for Percussion and Blockheads. Mog watched everything carefully. Perhaps he was beginning to learn something.

But no. As the men started to crawl off, Mog suddenly called, "Hey! Hey!" Brog almost swatted him from force of habit, but managed to pull up just short of Mog's blithely smiling head. The hunters turned back, and Brog flushed with embarrassment. He just didn't know what to do with the boy.

"Sun," Mog said, smiling at them all. They all smiled back. There was something pleasant about Mog. He was useless and crazy but harmless, and that was sort of endearing. "Sun," Mog repeated.

Brog had just about decided that Mog could use a little sleep tap, son or no son, when he suddenly noticed something very strange. Mog didn't look up or point or make any kind of gesture, but when he said "Sun," all the hunters glanced up at the big yellow thing. Brog realized that even *he* did it. He knew what Mog was referring to just from the mouth noise.

Mog picked up a stick and crouched down behind a large rock. "Sun," he repeated, and now he pointed to where the sun was, fairly high in the sky. He traced a line slowly upward. "Sun, sun, sun," he said, pointing higher and higher. Then he stabbed his finger straight up. "Sun!" he shouted and leaped out from behind the rock, stabbing wildly with his little stick.

He stopped and beamed at them. The men looked back, without comprehension, their mouths agape and a substantial amount of drool heading groundward. Mog lost his smile, and his brows knit together. Brog knew all too well how he felt, but he understood Mog's idea no better than the others.

Mog got down behind his rock again and gestured them to do the same. They looked at Brog, who decided he would not let anyone laugh at his son even if he *was* (clunk) in the head. He did a bit of tapping, and soon everyone was hunkered down, pretending to be behind a rock. Mog repeated what he had done before, and (with gentle urging from Brog) everyone repeated along with him, "Sun! Sun! Sun!" And pointed and jumped out. Then they stood there staring at each other. What did it mean?

Brog was dying of shame. "How can I ever live this down?" he was thinking. "They'll never follow my orders again. Of course, they don't follow my orders now, but still, this will make it even more—DON'T ATTACK UNTIL NOON!" All of a sudden, that idea was crystal clear in his head. Circle around the antelope, hide behind the rocks and don't attack until the big yellow—until the "sun" was directly overhead. That was what Mog was saying.

Brog helped Mog explain to the men. When Mog would say "Sun!" Brog would point straight up. When the men looked up, he'd whap them with his club. Mog's plan just needed a little positive reinforcement. Eventually, the idea got hammered into the numbest skull.

The hunters sneaked up on the antelope, a new sense of purpose in them. A plan! They actually had a plan! Quog was so excited he forgot to complain.

Since an exact time had been set for the attack, Brog could crawl around the perimeter and be sure each was in his proper place. Then they all waited, scarcely daring to believe that they actually knew what they were doing. They watched the big yellow thing climbing the sky. "Sun," each whispered to himself, watching the shadow of the grass grow shorter and shorter. When the sun reached its high point, almost as one man they threw themselves, shouting and waving their spears, down the slope. The antelope were almost completely encircled and the whole herd was killed, except for two that escaped through an opening. Drog had decided he was not going to tamper with his own personal formula for success, so he was sleeping behind his rock when the two antelope bounded over it, knocking the snores out of him with their hard little hooves.

It was the greatest hunt the Tribe had ever carried out, and they rejoiced all the way back to Here. Even hauling the eight carcasses up the long slopes wasn't so bad because they could imagine the astonishment of the women when they brought in the feast. And they wouldn't have to hunt again for days!

Although they still weren't sure exactly what he had

done, they all sang Mog's praises. All except Drog, who was made to carry the heaviest burden because of his laziness. He snarled behind his teeth and glared at Mog, as soon as he was sure no one was watching him.

4

"AARRGH!" (BURP)
[I THINK I WILL HAVE A LITTLE MORE, THANKS]

The women were running out of patience.

The men dawdled over the feast. And then they pretended even more reluctance than usual to act out the hunt. And then they did nothing but their usual strutting and preening.

It was enough to make you scream, but the women kept smiling and urging the men on. It was important. This hunt had been the most successful ever. The men had done something different, but what was it? The women needed to know. It wasn't that they didn't trust the men to remember on their own, but . . . well, yes, that's exactly what it was. Full stomachs tonight made for empty heads, and empty heads tonight made for empty stomachs tomorrow.

The men whirled and leaped and shouted and

pounced and generally showed off their astounding courage before the onslaught of the ferocious antelope. Even Drog joined in, unobtrusively. There was not yet quite such a thing as lying, but he was clearly ready for it as soon as it arrived.

When the men finished their playacting and looked to the women for approval, the women gave them a hard look that clearly said "And what else?" Quog jumped and jabbed and hooted and Shog beat his chest a bit more, but the women just kept staring, and finally all the men pulled into a sullen clump. It was rude of the women not to appreciate them more.

That was when Brog stepped forward. He had been strangely quiet all evening. Now he stood in the flicker of fire, and everyone, men and women, looked to him for the answer.

Brog pursed his lips and made a sort of hissing noise, then stopped and thought about it some more. "Gggrrarrgh!" he growled, just to clear his throat. Then he puckered his lips with an embarrassed expression and tried again.

"Sun," he finally got out.

Everyone looked up to where the sparks from the fire, yearning toward the star, vanished into darkness.

The big yellow thing had long before changed into the big red thing and slipped off the far side of the sky. But everyone knew what Brog meant by "sun" even though they couldn't see it, even though he hadn't pointed or even looked up. They saw surprise mirrored in each other's eyes. They all knew what Brog meant.

They didn't know what "talking" was, but they knew what he was talking about.

Brog stepped into the shadows and shoved Mog forward, all alone, to the side of the fire. The women started to laugh, but then they saw how serious and uncertain the men looked as Mog stepped forward into the ring of light where only mighty hunters had a place and where he had never stood before.

Slowly, Mog began to act out what he had done. It was hard for the women to understand that he was describing the hunt, since he didn't jump or growl or beat his chest. As they caught on, they looked at Mog in a new way, unsure but no longer just on the edge of a laugh. Seeing this, Drog stepped forward and said, "Sun," and pointed and nodded, as if *he* had had something to do with it. The other men joined in, jumping and hiding and shouting, "Sun," as if they could slay whole herds of antelope by the mere sound of the word. The women looked properly respectful (which cheered up the men a little), but they kept bringing their eyes back to Mog, who stood and waited until everyone settled down.

When silence had fallen, Mog reached down and picked up a rock. It was large and he struggled with it, but he finally held it up in both hands.

"Rock," he said. "Rock."

He dropped it, then sat on it to hide it. "Rock," he said. He looked at everyone.

They looked back.

Slowly, Brog walked to his son. He picked him up and set him to one side, then lifted the rock easily in one hand. "Rock," he said slowly.

"Rock," Mog agreed.

Brog gave a laugh and hurled the rock into the darkness where the cliff edge yawned, then put a hand to his ear to listen. When they heard it crash far below, he laughed and said, "Rock." He liked the word, it had a nice hard, growly sound to it.

Everyone laughed, and suddenly Drog held up a rock, announcing "rock" as if he had invented it. "Rock," Shog agreed, and reached for it, but Drog held on as if rocks had just become as scarce as words.

In a moment, everyone had a rock and was show-ing it off proudly. "Rock," each said to his neighbor.

"Fire," said Mog, pointing to the flames. A lot of forefingers got singed in the frenzy of pointing and repeating that followed. "Cave," he said. And "tree." And "bear."

Actually, he shouted that one, "Bear!" and pointed over their heads. "Bear," they all repeated happily, pointing behind them. "Bear!" he shouted again, and before they could respond, the large, hungry cave bear said, "Grrr!" which they knew meant "danger" with-out even having to repeat it.

This first vocabulary lesson ended in a mad scram-ble for spears and a good deal of dodging and running. Eventually, the monstrous bear grew tired of chasing these appetizing but speedy little morsels and ambled off. The men immediately returned to the fire and acted out the Great Bear Fight, glad to be the center of attention again and have the fireside all to themselves.

Drog had hidden in a cave during all the danger, but he tried to join in the display. Quog and Crog shoved him away from the fire, knowing he had done nothing. Angry, Drog suddenly made his eyes big and shouted, "Bear!" which made everyone jump and scramble for their weapons. Drog laughed and pointed at them. When they realized they had been tricked, the men proceeded to have a nice, old club-style conversation with Drog that didn't require any words at all. Drog didn't know it, but he had just invented the practical joke and been quite properly rewarded for it.

For the rest of the night, they danced and cavorted as usual, happy to forget about words and to be so admired by the women, who watched and thought their own thoughts.

Mog sat in the shadows and thought his as well.

5

"ROCK" (POINT)
[SUN]

The next morning they were all up early as usual, but Drog was up even earlier. When the Tribespeople came out from their caves, Drog was already at the High Cliff, stiff and sore but determined. He gravely gestured each new arrival into a circle with himself at the center. He meant to regain some of the glory he had tasted so briefly.

When Mog and his parents approached, Drog scurried onto the high point before anyone could stop him and pointed up to the sky. He spoke in the deep, serious voice he had been practicing all night. Just at that moment, the dawn broke in all its glory. It would have been very impressive, if only he hadn't pointed at the big yellow thing and solemnly proclaimed, "Rock!" He should have spent more time on meaning and less on tone.

Everyone was happy to help correct him. "Sun," they said, pointing to the object in question. "Rock," they continued, throwing many fine examples at him in an unselfish effort at remedial education.

That day they all watched the little son of the mighty hunter closely. He roamed about, pointing and saying things like "grass" and "water" and "dirt." The people were surprised to find that everything had its own mouth noise. They wondered how the little boy had discovered these secrets. It wasn't long before they realized they could communicate without using a club at all. You could say "water" when you were thirsty and "meat" when you were hungry. It wasn't exactly philosophy, but it made its point.

(For many years, however, a friendly swat with a club would still be considered polite in an old-fashioned way and bring a tear of painful nostalgia to the eye of many old-timers who never could get used to youngsters who just walked up and made noises at them.)

Brog's little son made quite a name for himself, and that name was Mog. He pointed to himself and said it. They were surprised that a person could have a noise, too. They were amazed when he tapped their shoulders and told them their names. They had lived all their lives without even knowing that they *had* names, much less what they were.

Some of the Tribespeople felt uncomfortable that the little boy (or "Mog," as they said reluctantly) could make a noise and everyone immediately knew he meant them. Names for things was obviously useful, but names for people? They might not have caught on except for something invented by Drog, who was finally getting the hang of twisting Mog's creations to his own purposes.

Drog was not happy with his name. It didn't sound nearly good enough for someone with his many fine but unappreciated qualities. You had to stick out your lips and make a funny face when you said it. This gave Drog an idea. He looked around to see who wasn't there to defend himself, then said, "Shog!" and made a funny face, sort of round-eyed and vacant, the way Shog sometimes looked. Several people laughed. Drog, encouraged, said, "Quog!" and twisted up his face into a whiny little pout. More people laughed. Drog hopped on one foot and rubbed the other while he pretended to cry. That brought even more laughs. Drog could say any name, and everyone instantly recognized who was being made fun of. They all knew this was not a very nice thing to do, but it still made them laugh.

Twenty minutes after "names" were born, their evil twin, "gossip," followed them into the world, and as a result, names were considered an unqualified success.

6

"—" (ſHOULDER TAP)
[GIRL]

Mog didn't know where the names came from. He just looked at something and he knew how to say its name. It was his gift, it was what he had instead of being big or strong or agile, and it was nice to be appreciated for it. He liked saying names, especially new ones. So it hurt when the Tribe stopped paying attention.

For a while, the life of the Tribe (as Mog informed the people they were called) was idyllic. Hunts went quickly and efficiently with Brog ordering, "Shog: rock. Trog: tree. Quog: (clunk)." The only difficulty was that they had to find game before "noon" ("Sun!" [point straight up]), because twenty minutes to one wouldn't be invented for a long time yet.

This left plenty of time to follow Mog around and repeat his latest words. But in a world of caves and rocks there are a limited number of things you can point at. Soon, the Tribe decided they would rather spend their leisure time in conversation than education.

"Grass," said Shog, and they all looked at the grass.

"Rock," added Quog, and they all admired the rock.

"Tree," Trog commented sagely. They all nodded agreement, those that were still awake.

Mog tried to regain their interest by doing subdivisions of things he'd already named. "Man" and "woman" and "boy" and "girl" were accepted and considered useful. They didn't object either when Mog started doing variations on "rock": "stone," "boulder" and "pebble" came in handy sometimes. But then Mog started on names for really big rocks that weren't quite boulders and medium-sized rocks with red streaks and small rocks with a bulge over on the side that looked like . . . Well, this was too much for the Tribe, which felt that "rock" covered all that very nicely. They ignored Mog's new words. And they mostly ignored Mog, who was growing bigger (not big, but bigger) even as he shrank in the Tribe's opinion.

So Mog was happy when something new showed

up one night, something that had to have a name. Not just something—some*one*.

It happened at the great fire. The men were dancing out their latest hunt with shouts of "Rock!" and "Sun!" and "Antelope!" and the women were pretending to be impressed.

A strange little girl.

She was just suddenly *there* among them by the fire.

She looked so different from the Tribe. Her face was dirty, her hair was wild and her furs were filthy and unkempt. Well, actually, that was the part that *wasn't* different from the Tribe. What then made everyone growl and shrink back from her?

It was her expression.

No, her expressions.

She looked at the circle of hunters with narrow-eyed watchfulness, at the huddle of women with open yearning, at the fire with wide-eyed delight, at the meat with hunger. Not just hunger, HUNGER! All of her expressions were overwhelming, ferocious. The intensity of her eyes could warm you or burn you, almost at the same moment. It was quite exhausting to watch her face.

Drog started to shrink away but caught himself when he realized how small she actually was. This girl had to be from one of the other tribes, thrown out or abandoned, and if she wasn't even good enough for one of those inferior groups, why should she be accepted here? Drog stepped boldly forward but froze when she shot him a look of challenge that changed quickly to contempt as she took his measure.

For a moment, everything was still except for the girl's eyes, which flashed here and there without pause.

Mog walked up to her happily. He cared nothing for tribes. All he knew was that here was someone new to name and someone new to learn the names. He felt useful again, and he smiled at her.

She looked at him threateningly, then warily, then uncertainly, then twitched her lips in strained imitation of a smile.

Mog tore off a chunk of antelope from the spit over the fire and held it out to her. She leaped forward with a speed that made the largest of the hunters flinch back. The food was sliding down her throat in an instant.

"Meat," said Mog.

Her eyes met his, while her mouth did not stop

ripping and chewing. "Meat," he repeated proudly, pointing at the fast-disappearing chunk.

"Fire," he said, pointing appropriately. And "cave" and "rock." The girl watched intently without slowing the passage of food through her mouth.

"Mog," said Mog, pointing to himself. He said it carefully several times and gestured an invitation to her, but she didn't stop chewing, didn't stop staring. Mog went around the fire, naming everyone. They weren't sure they liked this. It seemed doubtful such a wild-eyed little creature could speak; but if she could, none of them wanted his name to be the first in that voracious mouth.

Finally, she finished eating and threw the bone into the fire. She licked her fingers carefully and wiped them on her furs. She sat, then tossed her head and cleared her throat. "Meat," she said, in a strong, clear voice. "Fire, cave, rock, Brog, Pog, Shog, Quog . . ." She threw her glance rapidly around the circle, naming each correctly, and finishing with her gaze again on Mog. His was the only name she hadn't repeated.

"Mog," he said, touching his chest again.

She said nothing but watched, still questioning him, still waiting for something. Hunger burned bright in her eyes, and it had nothing to do with food.

Mog knelt in front of where she sat and put his hand on her shoulder in his naming gesture. The Tribe leaned forward to hear what the name of such a barbaric little creature would be. But Mog looked into those hungry eyes and his gift told him nothing. Or, perhaps, too much. Touching her shoulder, he felt her trusting, waiting, and many thoughts came to him, but no names. Finally, he just said, "Girl."

The Tribespeople were disappointed and yet not surprised. This proved other tribes were no better than animals if they didn't even have names.

The little girl didn't repeat the word, but some of the light went out of her eyes. She lowered them to see his hand on her shoulder, and then her head dropped onto her chest and in a moment she was snoring.

Mog drew his hand back carefully, then brought his mother to the little girl. Pog was surprised and not at all sure she wanted anything to do with this wild child. But she was a good woman and very proud of her Mog, so she carried the little girl off to their cave and made her a little sleeping place.

Everyone was unsettled that night, wondering if an idiotic and outcast child should be allowed into the bosom of the Tribe. They couldn't sleep because they worried what sort of a creature she might be.

Mog couldn't sleep because he couldn't wait to find out.

7

ſILENCE

Mog awoke at first light, meaning to wake the strange little girl and get on with teaching her the names. But she was already there, waiting impatiently for his eyes to open.

He led her around, pointing and speaking proudly. She said each name exactly once (all except his), then looked impatiently for what was next. She didn't seem the least bit appreciative, didn't realize how extraordinary his words were. She just followed him around, silently demanding more.

Mog grew tired and discouraged as he ran out of names. There had always been too many words for the Tribe, but there didn't seem to be enough for the little girl. He tried to walk away from her, to ignore her, but she followed him everywhere, her silence more demanding than any amount of speech could be.

Finally, Mog was so worn out that he threw himself

down for a nap beside the little pool where the men idled while the women worked. He tried to sleep, but even through his closed eyelids he could feel her waiting, unsatisfied gaze on him.

The men watched the strange little twosome with much laughter. Mog and the little girl were both (conk) in the head. They were a good match for each other.

Drog decided to show off how much smarter he was than this little girl by starting a conversation. "Grass," he said, pointing and looking around for approval.

"Grass," said Shog, who was always happy to agree.

"Tree," put in Trog. It was his favorite word, since it sounded something like his name.

"Rock, rock, rock," said Quog, pointing out several fine examples. He specialized in rocks, since it helped him be aware of what he might trip over in the immediate vicinity.

It was a fine conversation, and the men were proud of themselves, but the little girl ignored them.

Pog decided it was time to take over the little girl's

education. Names or no names, women had work to do. She pulled the little girl away from Mog's side, over to where the women were working on the previous day's hunt. She showed the little girl how they used a sharp rock to strip the skin from the meat, then how they scraped the furs and dried them in the sun, how they cracked the bones and made needles from the slivers. The little girl learned very quickly and did everything very well.

Once.

The little girl had no more interest in repeating chores than in repeating words. She was always hungry for more, but never more of the same. Since women's work was largely repetition, this was of little use.

When the little girl dropped the scraping rock for the tenth time and headed back to check on Mog's nap, Pog decided it was time to turn her attention to the area of personal hygiene. She picked the dirty little girl up in her arms and carried her to the pool.

"Bath," said Pog.

"Blub," said the little girl as she disappeared with a splash.

All the men laughed. They knew Pog's peculiar notions about cleanliness, and how Brog and Mog had to humor her by bathing, sometimes as often as twice a year.

The little girl shot right back to her feet in the shallow water, and the men were disappointed that she didn't seem angry at her dunking. It spoiled the joke. She looked thoughtful, as if this was a logical (although messy) part of the learning process. She watched the water trickling from her furs, then raised her head to gaze resolutely at Mog, who had opened his eyes at the sound of the splash. She smacked her hand on her chest, then placed it on her own shoulder in Mog's naming gesture. She glared at him, silently.

"Girl," he said, scowling at her. She had already said that word. Once.

She scowled back, then held up her arms and very carefully looked at the drops cascading from them. Then she touched her shoulder. Then she pointed at everyone sitting idly on the banks and touched her shoulder again and stared at Mog.

Drog nudged Shog and tapped his temple. "Mog,"

he said, and Shog laughed. The little girl certainly was "Mog" in the head.

Mog stood and walked toward the little girl. An idea was stirring. Were there other names? Names not just for things but for . . . things about things? He couldn't even think the thought because he didn't have the words yet to think it with.

He looked at her and all the water dripping off her. He looked at the others with no water dripping from them.

He pointed at the little girl. "Wet," he said.

The men were confused. "Girl," Shog said, in a rare dissenting opinion.

"Wet," Mog repeated, definitely. Then he pointed at the men on the bank. "Dry," he said, and laughed with delight. "Wet," he repeated happily, and "Dry."

Drog was suddenly scowling down at him. "Wet, dry!" he imitated in a whiny little voice. "Wet, dry!" He turned back to the others and tapped his head again. "Mog," he said scornfully.

Brog began to rise at that. Even if Mog was being strange, he wouldn't let Drog bully him. But the little girl was there before him. She slapped a hand on Drog's shoulder and shoved her face into his. "Dry," she said, quietly. Drog leaned back from her, not liking to be touched by this wild creature. She gave a sudden shove, and he went over backward into the pool. "Wet," she said, definitely.

The men roared with laughter at Drog, who came up properly sputtering and fuming. "Dry," they would repeat, patting themselves proudly. Then they'd kick more water at Drog and yell "Wet" into his crimson face.

The little girl suddenly pointed at Drog's twisted expression, then at the laughing faces around the banks. Mog nodded. "Angry," he said, pointing at Drog. "Happy." He pointed at the men.

"Angry, happy," the little girl repeated with the men and the women who now joined the group.

She strode bravely up to Shog and looked a question at Mog. "Bold," he said, and "Cautious."

"Cautious," Shog agreed, approvingly.

The little girl stood next to Brog and looked up at him. "Little girl," said Mog. "Big Brog."

The Tribe murmured its wonder. There could be more than one name to things. "Little girl, big Brog," they all repeated.

Mog held up a pebble. "Little rock," he said. The Tribe gaped. Could different things share the same word?

"Big tree?" Trog asked, pointing upward, and Mog nodded.

Drog lay in a sodden lump, exhausted and humiliated. The little girl ran a quick circle around him and back to Mog. "Quick girl," Mog said, and put his hand on her shoulder. When he said, "Lazy," everyone laughed and shouted, "Lazy Drog!" before Mog could finish his words.

Mog spent the day creating new words, words for moods, words for expressions, words for the ways you feel. Whenever he could think of nothing new, the little girl was there to push him forward.

The Tribe was excited again about these new words. Who would have thought there were names for things that you couldn't touch or see? These weren't useless like some of Mog's recent ideas; these were words you could use to talk about other people, and that was always entertaining. And for every word for the Tribespeople, Mog found three more for the little girl. He couldn't find enough words for her.

But that was the problem: he couldn't find enough words for her. She heard all his words and was never satisfied.

She was frustrating and unrelenting and inspiring.

8

HUNTING

The little girl joined the hunt the next day. This was an absolutely astonishing thing for a girl to do, and it surprised absolutely no one. She took the little practice spear that Mog never used and pulled him along in her wake, although he would have preferred to stay Here and make new words. But she was determined, so he shrugged and marched off behind the strange little girl. (Mog had created "strange" for an odd-looking insect, but Drog used it on the little girl and it stuck.)

The hunters started to object to her presence, but she glared at them and that was the end of that. She was unlike anyone else, so it was hopeless to try to make her follow the rules. Besides, they were happy playing with their new words.

"Long grass," said Crog.

"Tall tree," said Trog.

"Hard rock," said Quog, rubbing his most recently stubbed toe.

As they walked, the strange little girl used a rough rock to shape her spear. She scraped at bumps and irregularities and worked to sharpen the butt end of the spear as well as the point. The other hunters laughed to themselves. She obviously did not know how to handle a spear. A spear was used for jabbing, or sometimes you would plant the butt against something to brace it against the charge of a big animal. Either way, you didn't want a point on the end that you had to handle. And you didn't want to make the shaft any thinner than it already was, as she was doing. But she continued to make it thin and straight and sharp.

When they got into the plains, they came upon the track of a wild pig. This was good eating, but also more dangerous than chasing antelope. When they found the pig at a wallow, Brog gave soft instructions.

"Trog: tree."

"*Tall* tree," Trog amended proudly.

"Tall tree," Brog agreed, pointing high. When Trog looked up, Brog clobbered him with his club. No one else felt the need to improve on his orders.

The strange little girl stepped forward, slapped herself on the chest and waited for her orders. Brog was annoyed, and some of the men giggled. He gestured behind them and snapped, "Grass." The girl's brow knit at that, but she slipped silently into the grass as the others moved to encircle the pig. Mog didn't have to wait for orders to hide well away from the action.

It was a big boar, its twisted razorback as high as Brog's shoulder. Every man would have to do his part. When the men had had time to reach their places, Brog stepped out and confronted the hairy beast.

Its head whipped up at the first whiff of man-scent, and it turned its piggy eyes this way and that until it saw the man with the club and then the others approaching with spears from every side. It heaved itself up out of the mud and looked for the easy way out, but there was none. Its tusks ripped angrily at the dirt as it turned this way and that.

Then suddenly it charged, straight at Brog. He braced his feet and raised his club, but the wily old boar veered at the last moment, swinging toward the other hunters who, unprepared, scurried out of his way. The path was clear and the boar took to his heels. He was no antelope, but he was more than fast enough to escape the Tribesmen.

Suddenly, a thin shaft came flying from the nearby grass and lodged in the boar's hindquarters. It was not a killing blow, but it stopped him and made him swing around to snap at the sudden pain. Brog and the others leaped forward and used the delay to bring him down.

When the pig was finished, Brog pulled the thin shaft from the body. It was Mog's useless little spear. The little girl stepped nimbly from the high grass to claim it.

The hunters were amazed. A little girl bringing down a boar! Of course, she hadn't killed it, but just striking it in such a bizarre way was quite enough.

"Little girl!" they cried ("strange" little girl seemed disrespectful under the circumstances, even if it was more appropriate than ever). And "Spear!" And they made motions of hurling their spears at the boar. Shog got so excited that he actually threw his, but it wasn't shaped for aerodynamic flight, so it twisted and wobbled and didn't fly at all true, but did manage to give

Quog a good thwack on the shins. The little girl watched their excitement in silence and turned to look at Mog, who moved forward from his own place of concealment.

"Little girl!" "Spear!" Mog knew there was something missing here. If you wanted to express something, there had to be a name for it, even if it wasn't a thing, or a thing about a thing. She had done something. With something. To something. There were words for her and words for the thing, but what words were there for the doing? Could doings have names? You couldn't take hold of a doing with your hand and name it, but when you did it, you knew it had happened. And if you could imagine a thing, there had to be a name for it.

"Little girl," he said. "Throws."

"Throws," she agreed.

The hunters buzzed in wonderment. But Mog wasn't done.

"Little girl throws . . . spear," he finished.

They lapsed into a flurry of pre-Mogian grunts at that. They had no words yet for the amazement they felt. A dancing cave bear would not have surprised them as much as that first subject-predicate-object waltzing in their brains. They had thought the two-step of adjective and noun was as far as the dance could go, but suddenly Mog was showing them moves they'd never dreamed of. With the little girl his still-silent partner in the dance.

All the way up the hillside, the men shouted, "Little girl throws spear!" The women didn't know what to make of this, and the men refused to say more until the feast around the fire that night. They made the women really beg them to act out the hunt, and then all was explained.

By then, Mog had even more surprises for them. He named running and hitting and eating and drinking. And the Tribe practiced all these names and the corresponding activities until they fell exhausted into sleep or unconsciousness (depending on whether they'd concentrated more on eating or hitting).

Mog named everything he could think of. He even named naming. With each name, he would look to see if it was the magic word that would make the little girl speak more than the single repetition.

The little girl watched it all closely, fiercely. But she

said nothing. What did she want? What would make her talk?

Finally, Mog was tired out. "Sleeping," he named. And before he finished naming it, he was doing it.

9

HUNTING FOR WORDS

Time flowed on, and the Tribe was drowning in words. They could see that Mog would not stop inventing them until the little girl stopped frowning and talked to him, but no one could say when that would be.

First there had been nouns, then adjectives and verbs. Now, in the course of weeks, waves of adverbs and pronouns washed over them. Before they could catch a breath, articles and conjunctions came streaming in. Numbers, both ordinal and cardinal, were added to the mix. Each little drop seemed helpful on its own, but the flood of them all together was overwhelming.

The state of being was particularly hard for them to comprehend, the idea that even when you are doing nothing, you still "are." Drog was helpful at illustrating this concept, although it was often difficult to tell whether he was "doing nothing" as a concept or as a nap.

Mog was exhausted. He had thought that each new breakthrough would finally make the little girl speak her mind, or at least smile, or at least not frown so continuously. But she was always there ahead of him. Every time he came to an understanding, she was already gesturing impatiently toward the next idea he had not even known to exist.

Did she know what she was doing? Was she really leading him onward, or did he only imagine it? If she would only talk, only say his name. He tried to hold on to the sound of her voice from her single repetitions, but it always seemed just the echo of his own voice. In fitful dreams, she sometimes spoke to him, talked, said who she was and where she was from and why she tormented him so; but when he woke, he could never remember what she had said.

"You must eat more," Pog said by the fire one night. "You must sleep more."

Mog pushed the food away, his eyes locked on the little girl's.

He tried to explain to Pog his belief that she was silent because she had too much to say to him, that it was too much to put into the words she had. She would talk to him, tell him everything behind that silence, once he had given her all the words.

"There are enough words," Pog said to this. "We are proud of you and your words."

Mog shrugged it off. "She is always there before me. She knows the words are there when I do not. I just name them; she knows where they are."

Pog thought about this. "The scout finds the game, but the hunter kills it and brings it home. Without either one, we go hungry. Both should be proud. And both should eat."

But Mog and the little girl remained locked in their silent struggle throughout the meal.

"Me never see Mog so quiet," said Brog, who knew what he was doing with a club but was shaky with a pronoun.

"He's finally run out of words and can't think of any more," said Drog, who had done his part by inventing contractions out of sheer laziness.

The men rose to act out the latest hunt, which now involved as much talking (mostly flattering adjectives) as acting. The little girl joined them. No female had ever stood in their circle before, but no one bothered to say anything. Unheard-of things had become commonplace around Here.

She threw the little spear, then looked at Mog. She had done this repeatedly during the past week. Mog looked back in silence.

"The little girl throws the spear," suggested Shog. There wouldn't be any serious dancing until this got settled.

"That has a name," Mog said wearily. "And she knows it."

She ignored his words. She gestured to the remaining meat, threw the spear again, pointed at the meat, patted her stomach.

"The *strange* little girl throws the spear," Crog offered helpfully.

She ran to the edge of the cliff, pointed down to the plains. She dropped to all fours and walked slowly, then lay down and pretended to sleep.

"Antelope trip on rock and fall down," Quog said.

"Antelope die," Trog suggested.

The little girl breathed heavily.

"Antelope *sleep*!" Drog shouted. "Sleep! I'm good at this!"

Now the girl pointed toward the eastern sky and then traced an arc to a point overhead. "Sun!" several voices called. They were beginning to enjoy this game.

The little girl threw the spear again, toward the cliff edge, then gestured again at the meat. The happy guesses died quickly. What did it all mean?

Suddenly, Mog was standing next to her. His eyes were gleaming, either from the fire or the reflected intensity of her gaze.

"The little girl throws the spear," he said thoughtfully. "We eat the food. The little girl throws the spear. The antelope sleeps. The sun rises. The little girl throws the spear. The antelope is the food."

The Tribespeople looked at each other. The translation made no more sense than the charades had.

"The little girl . . ." Mog started again, and there were some growls of frustration before he finished with "*threw* the spear! She threw the spear and killed the antelope and it became food and we ate it." He laughed at the bewildered expressions around him. "And she *will* throw the spear. The antelope that sleeps now will become food and we will eat it. Now is the present, this fire, this meat, this throw of the spear. The past is the throw of the spear that killed the antelope, it's the food that we ate."

"The past gives me a stomachache," Quog said.

"Then you must eat less in the future," Mog

replied, "which is when the throw of the spear awaits the antelope that sleeps in the present."

As the Tribe buzzed, Mog turned excitedly to the little girl again. "Past, present, future. That is all there is, all there was, all there ever will be. You can't want more. Talk to me!"

She opened her mouth. All at once, she didn't look impatient or frustrated or angry anymore. She looked hopeful, then she looked confused. She closed her mouth.

Then she burst into tears and ran from the fire.

10

TENSE

The Tribe had never felt the need for anything except the present. Now they found themselves talking about what had happened yesterday and, even worse, what was going to happen tomorrow. Presently, with a little assistance from Drog, the past and future made them very tense.

Drog had always been surrounded by people who were stronger and braver and more skillful than he was. This was lucky for him, because it kept him safe and well fed. But it also worried him because, if he had been in their position, he would have thrown himself out to starve in a minute. So he always tried to trick his way into a share of the food, not realizing that the others were never fooled and shared in spite of knowing that he was lazy and weak and inept and a lot of other words that could be summed up by the name "Drog" and a knowing nod. People were basically kind rather than stupid, and Drog would never have believed that they shared not because of his cleverness but just because they were used to him.

Now he had the chance to repay all the Tribe's kindness by sharing in return the one thing he possessed in abundance—anxiety.

"It beautiful day," Brog said, one fine summer morning, stretching and yawning.

"It certainly is," Shog agreed, "and it is very good of you to share your thoughts on the subject."

"I ate too much last night," said Quog, "so I feel a little stuffy, but other than that it's a very nice day."

The men were stretched out on the grass by the little pool, enjoying their well-earned leisure, while the women cleaned and worked the skins from yesterday's hunt. In the old days, the men would have been out hunting every day that there was sun. Of course, the women still worked just as hard, even harder, perhaps, since there was more food to fix and skins to prepare, but that was *their* problem. If they couldn't work out a more efficient system as the men had done (with some slight help from Mog), they had only themselves to blame.

There was lots of scratching and burping and

lolling. The sun was up. There was plenty of food left from yesterday's hunt. What could be better? If the sun rises and there's meat for the spit, who would look beyond that?

Drog would, if he saw something to gain.

"Yes, it's a beautiful day," he said, sighing. "Too bad it won't always be so."

"What you mean?" asked Brog in a lazy, disinterested sort of way. He was chewing on a meaty bone left over from breakfast.

"I was just thinking about the snow."

"Snow?"

"You know, the white stuff that falls—"

"Me know snow. It pretty day today. Why you think snow?"

Drog shrugged. "I was thinking how deep the snow gets, and all this grass is completely frozen over."

"Yes, it get cold. Glad it not snow today!" A big smile bloomed on Brog's face, and he took a big, happy bite. There were nods and smiles of agreement all around.

Drog was smiling, too, but it was a thin and bitter smile.

"I was just remembering when the snow fell so

deep and we couldn't leave the caves for two weeks and when we did, there was no game to be found. The whole Tribe almost starved. Then we came across that mountain goat, and it would have given us one good meal." He thought very hard for a moment. "I think it was Brog who missed the stroke that let it get away."

Brog frowned in thought. Yes, he remembered, but it was just one club swing among hundreds, even thousands. And most of his efforts had brought food home for the Tribe. Why talk about that one?

A silence fell. The women had stopped their splashing and pounding to listen and think. Even in the heat of the sun, they shivered a little to remember.

Suddenly, Drog smiled. "I think it was Quog who fell in a crevice and found that frozen mammoth that fed us until the snow melted."

"Good old Quog!" called out Shog, and there were enthusiastic nods.

Quog looked a little confused, then smiled brightly. "I hit my head. It hurt a lot."

Everyone laughed and clapped Quog on the back and felt a little easier. Things always worked out somehow.

"It will snow again," Drog said. "Maybe even worse than before." That brought a cloud to the perfect day and started the shivers again.

Brog scowled and fingered his club. He was sorry that no one used clubs for conversation anymore; he still handled it a lot better than he handled words. "Why you think that?"

Drog shrugged, made a face to show he regretted having to bring it up. "Snow always comes again. Then rain and green things. Then hot sun and dryness. Then . . . snow again."

"Maybe not this time," Brog said. "Maybe it just stay warm until rain and green comes."

"That's right," said Shog. "No reason why not." But he didn't sound so sure.

"My feet get cold in snow," Quog said solemnly.

"We all get cold in the snow," Drog agreed. "And there'll be no food, and it will be very hard to live."

Brog saw that the women had all gathered around. "It beautiful day!" he snapped. "Why you talk about snow?"

"I know," Drog agreed, nodding sincerely. "It's strange to think on such a lovely day that the time will come when the snow will lie thick on this very ground, and there will be no dried meat left in the caves, and we'll go out into the cold, hunting all day for a single rabbit or some roots or anything at all to fill our shrunken stomachs. Today we have all we need, so we don't even have to go out and hunt. But tomorrow, or the day after, what about then?"

"When no food, we hunt more." Brog waved his joint of meat in the air.

Drog stared at the bone with its scraps of flesh. "But, eventually, the herds will move away again, and we'll think back about all the food we had today . . ." They were all staring at Brog's snack, and most were drooling as if they hadn't just eaten themselves sick. "And we'll wish that we had just . . . one . . . bit . . . left."

Brog looked around. They all looked as if they were getting up the nerve to grab his food from him. He started to stick it under his fur to save it for later, but suddenly Pog was there, plucking it unfinished from his hand.

"Go out and hunt," she said. "Get more food before the snows come."

He was amazed. "Feel sun!" he said. "No snow! Plenty food!"

"Drog's right," Pog said, hating to admit it. "The time will come when we'll need all we can get. Hunt now!"

"But meat now not last till then!"

"We could dry it to make it last longer, the way we do when the snows come," Drog suggested.

Brog shook his head. "Not do till we have to. Me hate dry meat. No taste, too tough, too stringy. Like it juicy."

Pog pointed a finger at him. "When there's nothing else, you eat it tough and like it."

"But there plenty else now!"

"There won't be if you sit around all day doing nothing. Now go hunt!"

The men were poked and prodded until they set off, grumbling, down the hill. But the women kept Drog home since he had proved himself smarter than the other men. That might not be a high recommendation, but they wanted to hear his opinions about how best to prepare for the coming snows. It was decided to eat as little as possible from now on and dry the bulk of the meat to be on the safe side.

And Drog kindly agreed to keep the provisions in his cave and oversee the drying and storing so they could be sure to have enough. Drog might not have amounted to much in the past, but he was the only man—in fact, the only Tribesperson at all—who had shown the sense to think about preparing for the hardship to come.

Mog had invented the future. All of a sudden there was tomorrow and the day after and the day after that, and you could talk all day and never make enough plans to be sure of all those looming tomorrows. A big, deep, dark hole had opened across their path and however many words were thrown into it, they just fell and echoed hollowly and never found a bottom. Once you opened up tomorrow, forever yawned beneath your feet.

Drog made it his job to fill that night-black void with all the worst things that could possibly happen— next week, or next month or when the snows returned. The women had always thought of the needs of the next few days, but this went far beyond that. Everyone knew the snows came every year, but they'd never had to think about it in advance before. When the time came, they'd wrap their furs tighter about them, and if there was little food, they'd just do without. It was a hard life, but it was usually pleasant when you weren't actually starving.

Now Drog's talk made them feel the pangs of that hunger even when they were surrounded by food. At the goading of Drog, the women urged the men to hunt more and more and to stockpile food against the winter. They were exhausted and hungry from their efforts, yet they couldn't eat their fill because most of the food had to be saved for the future.

And Drog reminded them of mistakes in the past. There had been a time when a missed spear thrust made you grunt with disappointment, then go on and forget about it. Now Drog reminded them of each past misstep that might have made the present better and the future less frightening. The silly but joyous fireside celebrations of the hunt were replaced with bitter critiques of faulty hunting techniques.

Who'd have thought it? Yesterday was just as awful as tomorrow, even though it hadn't seemed so bad when it was happening.

The memory of past mistakes fed fears of future starvation and made bellies rumble with present hunger. Mog had created possibilities, and Drog had turned them into fears. Squeezed through Drog's personality, forward thinking became pessimism and remembrance became regret.

II

CONDITIONAL HAPPINESS

Mog didn't notice any of this. He was too wrapped up in the declension of verbs to sense the declining spirits of the Tribe. He was so intent on new ways of speaking that Brog and Pog could scarcely talk to him. There was less communication than there had been before there were any words to do it with. And the little girl's gaze had gone from bright and ferocious to unfocused and tear-clouded. Silent as ever, she now helped Pog with the chores. She was remarkably capable at cleaning and scraping and cooking, but she was so tearful about it that Pog longed for the old days when she was bright and useless.

Mog's gaze was intense, but it was turned inward. He kept examining his grammatical soul for what was missing. He daydreamed often that she spoke his name, and he tried to imagine all that she would have to tell, everything she had stored up through the long silence.

It was a happy imagining, and he spent more and more time there, filling in the details of long, sunny afternoons babbling by the pool. He could imagine everything except what she would actually say.

It happened around the fire one night, where all the most important things seemed to happen. The meal was finished. It had not been as much as they might have wanted, but winter was approaching and they had to be prepared. So they sat listlessly, thinking about what they had to do before the snow fell, making the occasional bitter remark about some missed opportunity.

Mog was looking at the little girl, sitting quietly a little by herself. He imagined the fire that was once in her gaze, imagined it not angry but just as intense in its happiness. Imagined it turned on him.

He realized that this imagining had become more real to him than what he saw before him. How could a thing that didn't exist be so real?

And how could he put it into words? It was his only skill. It was his only gift.

She looked up to see him standing over her, silhouetted against the fire.

"If," he said.

She slowly stood. He realized suddenly that she had grown over the months since she first came to the fire. She was almost his height.

"If . . ." he said again, "you were to speak . . . I . . . would be glad to hear what you would say."

The Tribe watched them.

"What is this 'if'?" asked Brog. "You spoke, you speak, you will spoke."

"Will speak," muttered several voices.

"Spoke, speak, whatever," Brog snapped. "Past, present, future. Mog, you has never said 'if you were to speak' before. What is this 'if'?"

Mog continued to gaze at the litt—no, at the girl. At the person. "It is a way of talking about what isn't, what wasn't, what may never be."

"Oh, Drog already good at that," chuckled Brog. "It called 'lying.'" There were many laughs at that and Drog pretended to join in good-naturedly, but he wasn't amused.

"No, not lying," said Mog. "Picturing. Imagining. Dreaming. 'If' can make a dream almost real. I have imagined a place where the girl speaks, and I would rather live there than here. 'If' can take me there. And if she were to speak, there is nothing in the world I would want more than to listen."

He stepped to one side so the firelight would fall on her face. There was a new glow in her eyes, not anger, not anything he could name. But it thrilled him to see it.

She stepped forward slowly, thinking. She glanced at Mog, and suddenly she smiled, a dazzling smile, a smile that stopped his heart. A smile that said, teasingly, "Yes, that's it, aren't you the clever one." But it also said, "Thank you."

Then she stepped quickly to the fireside and looked around at all the Tribe.

"Once upon a time . . ." she said, very distinctly, as if she had always talked, and they had just never listened properly before.

The Tribe gave her all their attention, none more so than Mog. But it was an odd thing, like his dreams. He was so intent on the listening, on the joy of the simple sound of her voice, that he thought he would hold every word forever. But the tighter he gripped each word, the harder it was to grasp the next and when he reached out for another, the first slipped away. The harder he listened, the less he heard.

She told them a story, bright and clear as if she had

practiced her whole life for just this thing.

Her story was of a little girl who traveled by herself and saw amazing things and lived terrible adventures and came finally to happiness. And there was something about it that told them she was not talking about herself, yet there was something that said she was. And there was something more marvelous still which made them each think that she was talking about *them*, telling their own adventures and their most secret feelings.

Oh, it was a wonderful story, and I wish I could tell it to you as she did; but there was no way to save words then, so the story was told and then it was gone forever, except for what passed into the minds and hearts of those who listened. She was a much better storyteller than I am, so I would never presume to make up a story to put in her mouth. But it was a wonderful story.

You'll just have to take my word for it.

When she finished, as the Tribe sat in rapt amazement, the little girl walked shyly up to Mog and opened her mouth to pour out all that was unsaid. But Mog silenced her with a look as fierce as any of her own and turned and stalked away.

12

STORY TIME

There were stories every night now by the fire. The Tribe laughed and cried and clapped their hands in glee or terror, and they no longer called her "the strange little girl." Now, she was . . . the strange *bigger* girl. But at least everyone could say they loved her stories.

"I hate her stories," said Mog to himself. No, he admitted, he didn't hate them, but it made him mad that when she finally talked, it was to the whole Tribe, not just to him.

"No, that's not it!" he corrected himself. "That would be petty." It was that everyone loved her stories, when they were nothing but his words, put together in a particular order. Why should she get all the—

No, that sounded like jealousy, and Mog knew he wasn't the jealous type. No, let her go on telling her stories, and he would go on refining the rules of grammar. Someday she'd realize how much she owed him, and she'd feel sorry that she had snubbed him so badly. His rules were the only real difference between eloquence and a return to grunting.

"No, Grog, no!" he'd say, just trying to be helpful. "'Whom I hit,' not 'who I hit.'"

"Let's assume it's *youm* whom I hit," Grog would reply, suiting the action to the word and establishing himself as a particularly witty fellow. People took to carrying their clubs around with them again, in the hope that Mog would correct their grammar so they could say, "Let me get this straight: you who I hit (bonk); no, sorry, *youm* who I hit (conk); no, I mean youm *whom* I hit (plonk). Sorry to be so stupid, but thanks for the practice. Well, I've got to go, don't bother getting up."

Mog didn't grin, but he did bear it. "Someday they'll appreciate me," he'd say, between bouts of unconsciousness. And until then, the little girl—bigger girl—*whatever* she was—could just talk herself blue in the face, but he wasn't answering. He'd let her see how it felt.

And then one night, when trying to explain about dangling participles, he had been conked just once too often. Everyone had eaten their full ration, but it had gotten smaller every day. They were still hungry, and they wanted a good story to take their minds off it. The girl stood up and stepped to her place at the center of the circle as she always did, but suddenly Mog leaped up and called out, "Once upon a time!"

The whole Tribe looked surprised, including the girl, and that pleased him. Now she'd realize that they were his words, and there was nothing special about lining them up into stories. Anyone could do that. For a moment, he hoped she'd get angry (oh, to see those eyes flashing again!), but she stepped back quietly and gestured for him to go on. He turned to the others, half hoping for an argument there, but they sat in confused silence.

There was nothing for it but to tell a story.

All right, all right. She talked about little girls. He'd talk about something much more interesting.

"There was a little boy," he said, nodding his head to show this was going to be a good one.

"Who . . ." He stopped, trying to think what should follow.

"Are you sure you don't mean 'whom'?" called Drog, which produced some laughs.

"A little boy who . . ." Mog repeated, taking another run at his story. "Who . . ."

The word just hung there. Who could run. Who could throw. Who could jump. Who could eat, sleep, walk, talk, cough, spit, hunt, fly. Fly? A little boy who could fly? That sounded like an interesting story, and Mog found himself wishing the girl would tell it some time so he could listen.

He was staring at their eyes reflecting back the firelight. When *she* looked at these eyes, she opened her mouth and the stories came bubbling out; when he looked at them, he opened his mouth and his brain came dribbling out.

"Who couldn't even tell a story," Drog finished nastily, sitting back down and looking smug, as if telling a story was the simplest thing in the world. Certainly it wasn't as difficult as his job of rationing out a share of the hunt to everyone, with just a little bit extra for the man who was doing the hardest job.

Mog took a deep breath. "Who gave names to everything." The Tribespeople glanced at each other. They could already tell they weren't going to like this one.

Mog told his story, about a little boy who had a wonderful ability but wasn't appreciated for what he did.

To his credit, it was grammatically perfect. Every pronoun was in agreement, and not a single participle dangled anywhere, and there was some instructive use of the passive periphrastic.

What it didn't have was much plot, or adventure, or interest to anyone except the "fictitious" little boy who was the subject of it. Certainly not to any of the members of the "Group" who were his particularly stupid persecutors and who bore a striking (although, I'm sure, entirely accidental) resemblance to the members of the Tribe.

Oh, it was not a very good story, and I would tell it to you as he did, but I am a much better storyteller than he was (although not so good a grammarian), and I don't feel like trying to repeat what he came up with. It was not a very good story.

You'll just have to take my word for it.

Mog's story went on and on. The Tribespeople gradually trickled off to their caves. Even Pog, who might have stayed all night, reluctantly allowed Brog to pull her away.

Finally, there were just Mog and the girl, who never let her eyes waver from his. And the look in them was something like the look in Pog's eyes when Brog was making an obviously futile effort to rouse the sun in the morning. It was encouraging and hopeful and it held no doubt whatsoever.

Mog couldn't return her look. When there was no one else to face, he turned toward the fire and let his story trickle off into silence. He sank down there and sat with his head bowed, all of his thoughts drained away except for an overwhelming feeling of shame.

Mog stared into the fire, and the girl sat a little ways off, staring into him. Sometime during the night, when the wind grew cooler and the fire burned low, Pog came out and tucked furs around their still, sleepless forms.

13

AWAY FROM HERE

Very early the next morning, Mog woke from his waking dreams to find himself there by the ashes of the fire before anyone else was stirring. He saw the girl sleeping a few feet from him, and he wondered why she wasn't safely tucked in back in the cave. But then he wondered the same thing about himself. His memories of the previous evening were mercifully vague. He wasn't ready to let himself remember the full embarrassment of it, but he knew that he didn't want to be here when the Tribe roused itself.

He slipped quietly into the cave that had always been his home and found some dried meat to take with him. He paused by the still-sleeping Brog and Pog. He could scarcely see them in the predawn dimness, but he knew their breathing better than he knew his own. He would miss them terribly, and he knew they would miss him, but he wasn't going to stay where he wasn't appreciated, so he took a last look around before he slipped out of the cave. It was dark, dank and dismal. And home.

He rushed past the girl so he wouldn't pause again. After all, the whole mess was her fault, wasn't it?

He headed down the slope to the beginning of the great plains. His plans were a little shaky, but he thought he might bring the gift of language to a more appreciative tribe. Or, if that didn't work out, he would live on his own, with no irritating and unappreciative strange girls, whether little or big or absolutely medium-sized. Or he might just die all by himself if that seemed the most reasonable alternative, and then they'd feel sorry, assuming that they knew about it, which they certainly would if he had any say in the matter.

He had absolutely made his mind up, and nothing and no one could change it. He would hike far over the plains so no one would come running up to beg and plead and try to dissuade him. However, he was already hungry, since he hadn't had any breakfast before he left, so he decided it was best not to wait until he was really tired before reviving his strength, and there was such a pleasant spot beside the main hunting trail, and he was still absolutely resolved, so there was no reason not to sit right down and have lunch here just a few minutes away from the cluster of caves. Ha, just let them try to talk him out of leaving, he'd like to see that. No chance of that.

So he ate his lunch . . . slowly. He could imagine the Tribe waking up and realizing he was gone. The panic! The swiftly organized search parties, the desperation, the realization of how much they needed him. And the girl crying her eyes out when she realized she would never get the chance to speak her first words just to him.

Mog's lunch was dry, and no one happened to come by. It was really disappointing. He would have liked to show them just how absolutely definite he was about leaving and never returning. He could imagine the arguments they would give, his refusal to listen to their pleas, his anger and vindication at their tears.

He could imagine it, but he couldn't actually do it. Not without some cooperation. Where *was* everybody? He'd finished all the food he'd brought, and he'd eaten very slowly because he was a lot fairer than the Tribe members were and he would give them every opportunity to try to dissuade him (ha! just let them try!), but—but—where *were* they? Hadn't he been missed yet? He'd been gone all of—well, at least an hour or two, and they hadn't noticed his absence?

It was very depressing, and Mog thought about going back so he could hear tonight's story, which might cheer him up a bit before he set out tomorrow on the solitary remainder of his life. But it was unbearable to think of sitting around the fire with a bunch of people who didn't even realize that he had run away from them forever.

So he absolutely, definitely made up his mind and was just taking his first resolute step in a direction that was precisely halfway between running away and heading back, when the little—big—girl—person— when *she* stepped out from behind a rock and looked at him curiously.

This was the most attention he'd had from her since the stories began, except for last night, and he wasn't ready to think about that. For a moment, he almost smiled; then he remembered he was mad at her. He started to say, "I'm leaving forever—no, don't try to talk me out of it!" But then he remembered he wasn't talking to her.

So he waved a derisive farewell back toward the caves to show her he was going for good; then he squared his shoulders and stepped off down the path. Now she'd have to speak to him, she'd have to call out and try to . . .

She fell into step with him and fixed her face down the trail toward the plains. She was coming along! He cast one frantic look back toward everything he had ever known. He was suddenly actually leaving and he didn't feel at all prepared, but after a moment's hesitation, he sighed and matched her brisk pace.

They walked for hours under the bright sun.

He decided he wouldn't say anything until she did. She was the one who was too good to talk to him, so she had to make the first move. But she didn't. She seemed ready to walk forever without speaking.

So they walked. In silence. Mog grew tired and hungry and thirsty. He had never known there were so many steps to be taken in the whole world.

Late in the day she pulled him into a clump of trees. She moved a rock and uncovered a thin trickle of water. Mog dropped face forward into it.

As he sucked up the wonderful refreshment, he wondered how she knew it was there. Had she been here before? Did she know how much farther they would travel? Were they going somewhere that she knew? Then he realized that she hadn't drunk, that she was waiting patiently, turning her gaze in all directions as a lookout against danger. He quickly traded places with her and was too embarrassed by his thoughtlessness to ask any of his questions.

They sheltered there that night. She shook him awake at dawn. He stood stretching in the grass as the big yellow thing rose without any urging at all into a cloudless sky. Mog had never seen the sun rise anywhere but from the cliffs of Here—or rather, Back There. The sun was still well out of reach, even if they had been on the highest cliff.

He looked behind them, longing for a glimpse of the good old Tribe gathered on the High Cliff with Brog greeting the sunrise. Maybe they were thinking of him just then, wondering where he was watching the dawn and missing him. It put a big lump in his throat and gave him yet another reason for silence.

The girl selected a straight limb from a tree and shaped it with a sharp rock. (A weapon was another thing which Mog, of course, had not thought about. This running away was trickier than he had imagined it would be.) She crept up on a lizard, which was not Mog's usual breakfast fare, but he was hungry enough to allow some variety in his diet.

He realized it was lucky she was there to help him, and he quickly decided to forgive her all she had done to him in the past as soon as they got past their initial difficulty. She set out walking, with her eyes sweeping the horizon, unaware of how kind he was being to her.

That day they passed a high, flat-topped hill that was the most distant landmark that Mog had ever seen from the High Cliff on the clearest day at the farthest limits of vision. They moved beyond the horizon, across the plains and the hills beyond them and past the very end of what had been Mog's world.

Around noon of the third day, they came to a stream that was larger than any Mog had ever seen. The little spring and pool Back There where they cleaned and relaxed had seemed to him about as much water as you could ever see or would ever *want* to see in one place. But this stream was much wider and much faster. And much louder. Mog couldn't have been heard now even if he had spoken. He hadn't known that water could be so rude.

The stream dropped into a twisty, turny canyon, and they followed it for hours, unable to see beyond the next bend. Then suddenly it opened out, and the stream raced across a wide beach to lose itself in a great flatness that was very hard for Mog to recognize as water. It was bigger than he would have said the entire world was just three days before. And it didn't run like the stream, or lie still in its banks like the pond. It came and went, foaming upward, sliding back, flexing its muscles, breathing in and out. An unimaginably large, living thing that he would have fled in an instant if the girl (who seemed bigger in his eyes every moment) hadn't looked upon it calmly, even with pleasure.

He finally walked forward slowly to discover the wetness of it and took it up on his hand to feel the puddle and the drip of it. "Water!" he said to himself, then glanced hurriedly at her to be sure she hadn't heard, so it wouldn't count as his first words to her.

Once he knew what it was, he was glad he hadn't run in fear from this glorified moisture, no matter what its size. Before she could stop him, he scooped a handful into his mouth, then spent a long time spitting and ignoring the smile the girl could not quite keep off her face.

To show that this water, however big and bad-tasting, could not get the best of him, he waded out up to his knees, just like in the pool Back There. A mound of water suddenly rose up and knocked him end over end. He tried to get out of it, but up and down had become as mysterious as everything else about this overblown wetness. Finally, the girl caught his foot and dragged him, coughing and sputtering, onto the beach.

She led him back to the stream and motioned him to drink there. He wasn't going to fall for that one again, but then she drank to show it was all right and he followed her example. The water was sweet right down to the place where the great water foamed up to greet it. Mysteries on mysteries.

Mog felt he had discovered about enough for one day, but he let her lead him into a huge cave that another stream had carved into the cliffs near the water's edge. At this point, anything would be better than further dealings with the great water.

It was not like any cave he had ever seen before, which did not surprise him, since nothing seemed like anything else anymore. Caves had always been dark and damp, and this was certainly damp (it had a stream running through it, after all), but it was anything but dark. Glitters of sunlight bounced off sea and stream and were thrown far back into the cave, making shining wiggles of brightness that flowed and ran and flickered on everything. Deep shadows were replaced by magical dancing lights that shimmered a moment and then skipped away. The lights were everywhere, so solid in the corner of his eye, so liquid and fleeting when he tried to fix them with a stare.

Mog looked down at the lights twining and flickering over his hands and his body. He laughed to see himself awash in the light. Again, he couldn't tell up from down, but this time it was good and he felt himself swimming in the light, without knowing what it was to swim.

Then he looked at her face aglow, the light glinting on the roundness of her cheeks, playing over her smile and bouncing back bedimmed from the greater brightness that shone in her eyes. In that moment, he stopped missing Brog and Pog and everyone and everything he had known and left behind. He was completely happy just to be with her. Suddenly, this was the only Here he could imagine. He was swimming in more than light or water. He was swimming in love, a thing without a name because he had never known it to name it until that moment.

It was a magic place, and he suddenly knew that his greatest wish was about to be granted. Her eyes went wide, and she opened her mouth and she was going to speak. Finally. Just to him, no one else. He leaned forward to catch her first words.

"Mog, look out!" she screamed.

Startled, Mog stumbled back, tripping and falling. The girl was doing something similar in the opposite direction, jumping back and falling, and he was just wondering if she was as shocked by her words as he was, when the white belly of the big long-toothed cat went sailing over him. It seemed to take forever to pass overhead, short white fur laid flat against the taut, rippled muscle of stomach and haunch. He could see every hair on the legs and the paws and the . . .

Claws, he saw the claws, the great, flexed claws, and everything speeded up again.

He scrambled to his feet as the huge cat landed and twisted back toward them, growling now that the surprise was gone, a deep, terrible hungry growl that seemed to have his name in it. The mouth was wide, the fangs glistening and as sharp as the sabers that wouldn't be invented anytime soon. Between those gleaming daggers, the throat was red and ribbed, and

Mog might have slid right down it to the source of those rumbling growls that vibrated through his whole body, but the girl had his arm now and pulled him backward into the stream before the cat could unscramble its mighty paws for another leap.

The water washed over Mog's head, but the girl caught his hair in one hand and thrashed with the other hand and both feet to pull them toward the narrow ledge which was the opposite bank. The stream was not very wide, which was fortunate since Mog seemed determined to inhale as much of it as possible. When she dragged him up onto the ledge, he coughed and spat and retched until he could breathe again. On the other bank, the big cat did its own coughing and spitting, but it was rage that filled its innards, not water. It stalked the stream's edge and burned them with its eyes, every now and then letting a paw touch the water to see if it had gotten any drier.

Suddenly, Old Long-Tooth swung his muzzle toward the cave entrance. His nostrils flared. He smelled other prey nearby. He turned back toward Mog and the girl and looked at them carefully, remembering them. He never forgot a meal until he had eaten it.

And then he was gone.

Mog would have been happy to stay on the little ledge until he knew they were safe, but he wasn't sure of the average life span of a long-tooth, and the girl had already started back across the stream.

"Let's build a fire," she said, "before Long-Tooth thinks about coming back." Quickly, they gathered dry driftwood and started a little blaze, then settled down to dry out.

"I'm sorry," she said, when they were finally comfortable.

"For saving my life?" Mog asked.

"That those were my first words to you. I wanted the first time I spoke your name to be perfect. I thought in this special place I could find the words. To thank you for your gift. But then out they came without thinking and all they were was 'Look out.' It's disappointing."

"Being dead would be disappointing. Being alive is good. I'm glad you didn't wait for a more auspicious occasion." Mog suddenly realized that they really were talking, finally, and it was as easy as he had hoped it would be. "And now we've got the first words out of the way, so we can just say anything."

Which they proceeded to do. For days at a time. Like starving people brought to a banquet table, they threw themselves into delicious, indiscriminate conversation, taking great bites of serious discussion and little nibbles of chatter and relishing it all with saucy banter.

At some point, he asked her, "Where did you come from? Why did you leave there? Why were you all alone?"

She shrugged and stared off into space. "I don't want to talk about it."

Mog tried again from a different angle. "The stories you told around the fire—did those things happen to you?"

"No," she said. "Not really. They were just ideas I had. But I couldn't get them out until you made up 'what if.' They were just imaginings until I had 'what if' to make them real."

"But where did your ideas come from?"

She smiled. "Where did your words come from?"

"Ah," he said. "There."

And they both thought about that place in the mind that was like a cave (but, on the other hand, wasn't anything like a cave), and they both knew they couldn't ever describe that place, even to each other. It was a good place, but it was a place where they would always be alone.

When they grew hungry for something besides conversation, the girl took Mog down the shore to a cove where the beach was filled with the eggs of sea turtles that had come there to breed and the shells of others that had come to die. None of the Tribe had ever seen a turtle before, but Mog quickly learned they were good to eat, as were the eggs.

There was another strange thing in the cove. When they first came, they saw Old Long-Tooth playing with a turtle shell at the very farthest end. It was a big shell, bigger than Mog, and the cat was flipping it over and spinning it on its back and peering into it and clawing at it. He paid them no attention, so they ignored him right back since the inlet kept them safely separated.

Mog and the girl soon made the cave into a cozy home. She twined thin vines into nets to drag through the shallows, and he learned how to use a spear in fishing, to hold the point beneath the water because it bent very strangely when it broke the surface, although it straightened out again when removed. It was one more strange thing about this strange place, but he decided he could accept a little strangeness if it came with so much happiness.

They were content. They had what they needed. They had all the words in the world, and they delighted in giving and receiving them. They were together.

And they lived happily ever—

14

*J*HELL GAME

Well, no, of course, they didn't. Not *ever* after. That only happens in stories, and yes, I know, this is a story, but it's not going to happen in this one.

Real life is never put together as well as a good story. We might all do well to try to get born into stories instead of the real world. (As long as we're the heroes, that is.) In a story, the hero triumphs and gets the girl and says something clever, and that's the end. In real life, it never happens that way.

No, there were problems to come—big problems—and I'll get to them. But I wanted to give Mog and the girl a few paragraphs to enjoy a little peace and quiet before I started making their lives difficult again.

Which Drog was already doing. You remember that large turtle shell the saber-tooth was playing with? Well, Drog had gotten himself into the unlikely and unenviable position of being inside that very shell.

How did he get there? We'll have to backtrack a ways to get the answer.

Back at Here, Drog had been very successful in his scheme to be in charge of preparation for the coming snows. No one else could imagine as many awful things as he could, so they just assumed that he also knew what to do about them. He didn't, of course, but he was perfectly happy to pretend that he did.

The major feature of his plan for facing hard times was to stay as personally well fed as possible. When the hunts returned, before the men could even start bragging, he directed the women to prepare a small portion of the kill for that night's meal and set the rest aside to be dried the next day. If, during the night, some additional choice cuts happened to disappear from Drog's cave where they were stored and if Drog's belly happened to swell by a similar volume, who could prove anything? Besides, Drog told himself, he was working very hard for the good of the Tribe, so he deserved a little extra. The price of Drog's eternal vigilance was Drog's eternal appetite.

But trouble was brewing. As the Tribespeople grew thinner, Drog grew fatter. Their stomachs growled from emptiness, but his groaned from overindulgence.

He didn't like the way Brog looked at him; he thought the big fool was just watching for him to make a mistake. (He could never have imagined that Brog was only yearning for the leadership that had slipped through his fingers.) All Drog had working for him was his imagination and his wiliness and his willingness to twist any good thing to his own purpose. He needed something more concrete to ensure his future.

So he watched Mog carefully. Drog had made good use of Mog's creations before. Now he hoped to find a secret that would solidify his power. He laughed to himself as he saw Mog slipping in the Tribe's opinion, becoming more and more of a laughingstock, all because he was too infatuated with his words and his girl for their own sakes. The only reason that Drog could see to care for something or someone was for what you could gain by it. He encouraged the Tribespeople in their poor opinion of Mog, even as he watched for anything he could use to his own advantage.

He watched from his cave when Mog sat staring all night after his disastrous attempt at storytelling, and he followed cautiously when Mog set out to run away; and, when the vicious little girl departed with Mog, he guessed this was forever. Drog had to make a quick decision; this was his last chance to get some use out of Mog, but there was a great risk. If he followed Mog and was gone for too long, he might lose his position with the Tribe, but he might find something that would give him power that even Brog would bow before; and if he stayed, let Mog go on his own, he might lose his position anyway, once they knew that he wasn't doing anything they couldn't do and was cheating them besides. Between sneaking after Mog and persevering on his own, sneakiness inevitably won out.

Drog ran back to his cave and stuffed as much food as he could carry under his furs and followed Mog and the nasty little girl across the plains and over the hills and down to the shore. What did he have to show for his efforts? Nothing but aching feet and a shrunken stomach, because he couldn't possibly carry enough food to satisfy his enormous appetite for any length of time, and when it came to hunting, he was even more helpless than Mog.

So when they went into the cave, he slipped on down to the shore, looking for food. Yes, everything was new and strange and wonderful, but if Drog couldn't use it to his advantage, he ignored it.

He found the turtle shells and kicked them out of his way without a thought. This happened to uncover some turtle eggs for lunch, which was the first good thing he had gotten out of all this.

He was licking the yolk off his mustache and looking back up the shore, wondering if he should give it up, go back and try to regain his position with the Tribe, when the long-tooth came slouching around the angle of the bluff, nosing at Drog's prints in the sand.

Drog turned and ran. There was no shelter ahead. There was no way up the cliffs. He had almost decided to run into the water and take his chances with drowning, when he tripped over a really big turtle shell. He heard the growls of the cat just behind him and, without thinking, shoved his head and shoulders into the neck hole of the shell. It took some wriggling. If he hadn't been starving for a couple of days, he couldn't have made it. But his new relative thinness made it possible, and the angry roar of the long-tooth provided wonderful motivation for that last good shove.

He pulled his feet in just ahead of the snapping teeth. He was twisted up and he was cramped and he was uncomfortable, but the cat couldn't get at him. It could squeeze about two claws through the opening, but it couldn't quite get its whole paw in to hook him. It could roar through the hole loud enough to make his ears ring, but it couldn't blow him out by sound alone.

Drog was just beginning to feel smug when the cat discovered the pleasures of Spin-the-Shell. The shell turned quite easily on its smooth bottom and even more easily when you flipped it over on its rounded top. This was a new game for Old Long-Tooth, and he was both entertained and hopeful that he might just spin out a tasty meal.

Drog, as you can guess, didn't enjoy the game nearly as much. He was soon dizzy and nauseous, and his head was spinning even when the shell wasn't. He had to keep braced so that a foot or an arm or a head wouldn't pop out of the neck hole and into the eager mouth of the big cat.

He soon lost his turtle egg lunch and last Tuesday's dinner and the remains of meals he couldn't even remember. Now he was messy and smelly as well as cramped and dizzy. Surely the long-tooth would get bored and leave him.

But Old Long-Tooth wasn't bored and wasn't

messy or smelly or cramped or dizzy. What he was was patient. And hungry.

Much later, the thoroughly sick and miserable Drog got a glimpse through the neck hole of Mog and the hateful little girl at the far end of the cove. "Look at them, Old Long-Tooth," he whispered. "So young, so tender, so delicious. Yum, yum, yum!" Old Long-Tooth cocked an ear. He had never heard such mouth noises from one of the two-legs before.

"Look at me," Drog went on, "all skin and bone." He almost stuck an arm out to show how skinny it was (which it wasn't, actually) before he realized the long-tooth might treat it as an appetizer rather than a visual aid. "Take my word for it," Drog confided, wiggling his chubby fingers from the safety of his shell. "You should be going after them, not me. Go!" he shouted, "you big, stupid, buck-toothed—"

The cat chose this moment to show who was the master at mouth noises. He shoved his fangs against the neck hole and dropped his jaw and let Drog admire his tonsils while he let loose a roar that made Drog's brain ooze down and hide behind his rattling teeth. Then the cat reared back, still in full roar, and gave the shell a swat that flipped it end over end. Drog braced himself to stay in the shell no matter what. Then he felt the water coming in and changed his mind. He squirted out of the neck hole and balanced himself on the shell as it sank into the great water. The long-tooth spat and hissed from the shore, but the big shell with the little Drog stuck to its back was too far out in the water.

Rising cold water is a wonderful inducement to good posture. Drog stood his tallest and managed to keep his head above water as the shell rocked beneath his feet, then settled into the sandy bottom.

He waggled his hands in the air and taunted the long-tooth. "Nyah! nyah! nyah!" he said, which was not a word even then, but summed up his feelings most effectively. Then a wave washed over him, turning his nyah-nyahs to glug-glugs, and he decided to keep his mouth shut.

They might have been there all day, but a sudden bleat made the cat turn its yellow eyes up to where a young, incautious antelope was gazing over the edge of the bluff. Old Long-Tooth swung his eyes from the tender young buck to the nasty, smelly, noisy thing in the water.

Drog saw something like a smile behind those twin

daggers, then the cat threw itself to one side and loped off down the beach toward a place where it could climb.

Drog stood on the shell in the water until the sun sank low. He had never felt secure, so standing on a slick shell with the water lapping his chin was pretty much par for the course. Then he threw himself as far as he could toward the shore and thrashed himself up onto the beach.

Drog was now wet, cold, salty, messy, smelly and hungry; he had wasted several days and had probably lost his soft position back home. It would certainly be understandable for anyone in Drog's position to be a bit disgusted with himself. But Drog was not just anyone, and the thought of being disgusted with himself never entered his head. He was disgusted with everyone else, with the Tribe, with the long-tooth, with the big water, with the turtle shells, and most of all with Mog and the repulsive little girl.

No, that wasn't really true. It was to Drog's credit that he considered himself a fair man (on the basis of absolutely no evidence), and he had to admit that he wasn't disgusted with the turtle shells.

In fact, he was rather interested in the turtle shells.

He couldn't think why, but some idea kept twitching in the back of his mind like an itch in the back of your throat where you can't possibly scratch.

He looked at them in all their sizes from tiny to huge, the mossy green backs of the biggest ones, the pale pastel of the smallest. He cared nothing for the lovely colors and the intricate patterns. But he suspected they could give him some advantage, and that was a very endearing quality.

He hid for the night in an uncomfortable cave that was too narrow for the wide shoulders of the longtooth just in case it returned, which of course it didn't (isn't that always the way when you're prepared for something?). Turtle eggs made a rich dinner and a hearty breakfast. He gathered many of the smaller shells together and strung a vine through them so he could carry them. Then he set off on the three-day trail back to Here.

15

CATCHING UP

Where things had happened in his absence.

First, there was the sadness for the missing Mog.

Which didn't last long.

That may sound terrible, but you have to remember that this was a time when you couldn't take a walk without seeing as many large carnivores as you would taxicabs today (and they didn't all disappear when it rained, either). With so many big, furry appetites about, you hoped the Tribe would all be together each evening when the fire was built, but there were many nights when one place or another was empty.

Oh, Pog shed her tears in private, and Brog followed Mog's trail until it disappeared into the trackless plain. Beyond that, there was nothing they could do except pause every now and then to sigh and wish they had given back to their clever son a few of his own words, like "glad" and "pleased" and "proud." The rest of the Tribe, too (now that he wasn't around to irritate them), had some good words for him, but they usually managed to forget that they wouldn't have had any words at all without Mog.

Then there was the loss of the strange little girl, as they still thought of her, although she had grown out of both littleness and girlhood. But she had remained unflaggingly strange, and that was both good and bad: good for the pleasure of her stories around the fire, bad (or at least uncomfortable) for . . . well, for pretty much everything else about her.

Then there was the loss of Drog, if loss was the right word. This would have been greeted with a shrug and a yawn except for his position as Food Divider. In trying to find a replacement for Drog, they discovered that the job required certain personal qualities that were lacking in most Tribespeople. These included ruthlessness, arbitrariness and lack of compassion. It seemed strange to value someone for such unappealing characteristics, but the job was almost impossible to do without them.

Several of the men tried dividing the portions, and everyone ended up full and satisfied. This was a sure sign the job wasn't being done properly. The women said, "We were never this well fed when Drog was doing the job." This was an odd sort of complaint, but Drog had finally come to be appreciated, and that for all his worst qualities (of which he had many).

Eventually, Brog took on the job.

A week had passed, and Mog was given up for lost. Brog had searched and mourned, and it was time to forget his private loss and get back to the Tribe. He didn't see the need for the Food Divider, but this might be his chance to regain his leadership of the Tribe. And since the others had shown no talent for the job, he felt confident that he could be as bad as any of them. Of course, the Tribesmen never complained to him, and, secretly, they were probably happy to get the extra rations.

One day Brog was carrying his portion of the hunt back to the cave. He always paused at the trail that led down to the plains and gave a good look to see if there was any sign of Mog. He would never admit to himself that was what he was doing since Mog was definitely dead and it was a plain waste of time to give him any further thought, but still he would pause and look and a figure would appear in his mind's eye that seemed younger and smaller and, if possible, more dear every time he looked. This slight figure (so vulnerable, so needing of his protection) was so real in his mind that it took several moments to realize there really was someone coming up the path.

Brog shook his head and blinked his eyes, but the figure was real. It was thin and halting in its steps, and he started to run toward it and open his mouth to call the name he'd thought he would never get to call again. But then the figure raised its head and gave him a hard, calculating look, and Brog held back, knowing it was a starving Drog who had returned to him. Trailing a string of shells behind him.

Drog had grown to hate the shells as he walked. He would pick them up and turn them over and over in his hands, looking for the use of them; and many times, lost on the plains, with no food or clear signs back to Here, he almost gave up and left them behind. But then he would think of Mog and Brog and the others, and the revenge he longed to have on them for all their unprovoked kindness (for there is nothing more unbearable for a man without tolerance than to be tolerated), and he would grumble and keep dragging the string of shells, figuring it was just one more burden that the Tribe had forced upon him.

Finally, the landmarks grew more familiar, and he

saw the High Cliff above him as he started up the last part. He was almost back to his cave, when he saw Brog standing at the head of the trail.

Brog still had Mog in his mind. "Drog," he called. "Where you come from? You see Mog anywhere you been?"

Drog was drooling at the haunch of meat that Brog carried, but he knew this was no time to reveal weakness. "Mog?" he asked, all innocence. "Is he missing?"

Brog shrugged, not wanting to talk about it now that his hopes were dashed. "Where you been? What you do?" he asked, to change the subject.

"I had things to do," Drog replied, puffing up his sadly reduced frame to seem as important as possible. He kept the shells hidden behind him. He still didn't know why he had dragged them so far, and he was a little embarrassed.

"Me do your job now, dividing hunt," Brog said. "No need you do anymore."

Drog shrugged to show it didn't matter to him. "I have other things to deal with. More important things." Brog tried to see what was behind Drog's back, but Drog stepped in his way, trying to be casual.

Brog didn't want to reveal his interest by asking.

"We have good hunt, kill bison. We take all risk, now you want share I very sure."

Drog tried not to drool or appear eager. It infuriated him that someone with such poor grammar should feel superior to him in anything, but he swallowed his feelings, which, bitter though they were, were all he'd swallowed in several days. He started to push past Brog, saying, "Excuse me, I'm very busy just now, no time for chatter."

Brog considered this rude and he would have said something, but talking was never as satisfying to him as doing, so he stuck out a foot and tripped the irritating little man. This made Brog laugh, but did nothing to improve Drog's mood.

Now Brog could see the turtle shells. He stopped laughing. "What you got there?" he asked, eyes aglow with curiosity.

"Oh, you wouldn't be interested," said Drog, gathering them up as if he were trying to hide them and go on his way.

"But me never see anything like them. What are they?"

"Of course you've never seen anything like them," replied Drog, "for I have the only ones in existence."

"But what their name?"

Drog started to say they didn't have a name because even Mog had never seen them, but then he
thought, why should Mog do all the naming? These
things were his and he would name them himself. The
shells were hard and green on the back and . . .

"Why, they are greenbacks, of course." As a name,
it wasn't much of an accomplishment, but Drog was
instantly proud of it and thought this naming was
easier than it had looked. And he knew he would
only get better with practice. "Yes, greenbacks," he
repeated happily. "I would have thought that even
someone like you who thinks of nothing but chasing
animals with sticks would know the value of greenbacks."

"But what they for?"

Well, that was the question, of course, that Drog
had been asking himself all the way across the plain
without ever getting an answer, but he certainly
wouldn't admit that. "Isn't it obvious?" he snapped,
handing one to Brog, hoping the hunter would dredge
some useful idea out of that tiny brain of his. But Brog
just turned it over and over in his hands, amazed. Drog
watched scornfully. The greenbacks were obviously of

great value, but Brog was too dim to see it. Of course, Drog couldn't see it either, but he didn't let that alter his low opinion of the hunter.

"What you do with 'em?" Brog asked.

"Why . . . why . . ." Drog shook his head and sputtered as if it were perfectly obvious. But he still couldn't think of any use for them, so he grabbed the shell back and snapped, "You don't do anything with them. They are far too rare and important for that. You just . . . gather as many of them as you can and . . . keep them." Drog wanted to kick himself (a desire that made him for just a moment more like the rest of the Tribe than he had ever been before). It was the feeblest idea he'd ever come up with, but he was stuck with it now and couldn't back down.

Brog thought about that, his brows knitting together, his mouth hanging open. "But no one in Tribe has any that me ever see."

"That's their problem, isn't it? The greenbacks are mine. I . . . own them." Drog barely stumbled over the word before he realized that it was another brand-new word. And a lovely one, too. "Own." What a nice thought. And this second one had come even easier than the first. This word stuff was a cinch! He'd soon show Mog who was boss in the word department.

"Own." It was something no one in the Tribe had ever done. Oh, you had your spear and your furs, but that was just because you used them all the time, and no one would think of taking them from you. And you might take a good hunk of meat from someone else, but that was just to eat it, not to keep it. The thought of having something just to have it, to "own" it, was brand-new, and it made Brog think even harder, which wasn't a pretty sight, involving as it did some pretty grotesque faces and a great quantity of drool.

"Say," Brog said, his face relaxing as a light shone in his eyes. "Me like 'own' one of those greenbacks. Where I get one?"

"I have the only ones."

"Well, give me one."

"Give you one? You—who were just saying how I didn't even deserve a share of the bison you killed?" Drog knew this was a critical moment. Brog might just slug him and take a greenback. Even take them all. There was a time when he would have done it without a moment's hesitation. But Brog, who was frightened of nothing, was nonetheless intimidated by words and new ideas. With luck, he might just . . .

Shrug his shoulders and say, "Me kidding. Me give you piece of bison. You give me greenback."

It was a victory, and Drog almost handed over the greenback and grabbed the meat before he thought. But there was more here to be won, so Drog sucked back a bit of drool and said, "Now, let's think about this. You're offering me just a small part of one bison. And there are about a million bison on the plains below." (There was no word for "million," but Drog wiggled his fingers a lot to indicate a whole bunch.) "And these are the only greenbacks anywhere. Does that seem fair?"

"Me give . . . whole bison for one greenback," Brog said. "You take this, and me get you rest from what we have in cave." This would take a substantial amount of his and Pog's reserves, but he had to keep up with Drog if he wanted to regain his position in the Tribe. And somehow the idea of not "owning" a "greenback" had become intolerable to him, even though he had never heard of either word five minutes before. Mog was gone, but greenbacks were here, and it was suddenly important to hold on to whatever he could. The world was racing away from him, and he thought he might never catch up with it.

Drog hesitated, mentally trying out a disparaging comment about dried meat versus fresh, but the look in Brog's eye said he had reached the end of his bargaining abilities and the club was the next tool he would employ. So Drog agreed, handing over a greenback with great ceremony and telling Brog he would go now to his cave with his other greenbacks and wait for the delivery of his bison. Brog nodded happily, turning his greenback over and over in his hands.

As Drog slipped away, he heard Grog calling, "Hey, Brog, what you got?" And Brog answering, "You don't know greenback when you see it? Boy, me sorry for you!"

Drog smiled to himself. Without realizing it, Brog had become his employee. Hey, there was another one of those new words! It just got easier and easier when you were as smart as Drog.

Pog wasn't convinced when she first saw a greenback. Sure, it was pretty, but what was it for? And a whole bison? It looked as if their first big argument was brewing, and she was going to demand that he get their bison back. But then Clog, who was the wife of

Grog, dropped in to brag about the beautiful green-back she had and how it had only cost two antelope. Brog was just leaving to return his greenback to Drog, but Pog grabbed it from him to show it off to Clog, who pretended to be happy for her but was clearly embarrassed to see that Pog's greenback was bigger than her own. When Clog left, Pog turned to Brog with a bright look in her eyes. "Where can we get more greenbacks?" she asked.

That's how Drog came into power he had never dreamed possible.

16

HOMECOMING

The long summer fell into autumn, then wandered into winter, and the two young people lived on by the sea. They did not travel to the turtle beach since the turtles wouldn't return until summer, so they never saw evidence of the schemes Drog had hatched after he came out of his shell. They stayed in their cave and along the shore nearby. They learned to catch the other creatures that lived in the water and always kept a wary eye out for Old Long-Tooth. Sometimes they were hungry and sometimes they were cold, but they were together, and that made all the difference.

I should say that neither one of them was little anymore. We wouldn't call them grown-up today, but that's because we're lazy and take our time about it. In those days you had to grow up long before you'd grown, if you take my meaning.

Oh, yes, and they were married.

Well, not married, exactly. There was no license

and no blood test and no extravagant church wedding that left both families not talking to each other for years afterward since Uncle Louie must have spiked the punch, because that was the only reason that Cousin Henry would have danced with that lamp shade on his head.

No, there had been nothing as solemn and meaningful as all that. There was just the simple feeling that they would stay together forever. It was very unconscious and not at all solemn. In fact, it made them quite cheerful, and the thought of not being with each other never even entered their heads. For them, being married wasn't an act; it was a fact.

"Why have you never given me a name?" she wondered aloud one night as the cozy glow of an embered fire held off the cold darkness beyond. The soft accompaniment of unseen waves made music of her words.

"How could I name you?" he replied. "A name is for those that are one thing. A rock is a rock, Pog is Pog. And a name is for those that are not another thing. A rock is not a tree, Brog is not Drog. But you are too many things to be just one. And just when I think I know the lot of you, I find something else that you are.

How could I limit you by one name? Would it be Pretty? Or Fleet-of-Foot? Or Good-with-Your-Hands. You are any and all of those. But you are also Story-Teller. And Too-Smart-for-Me. And Auburn-Hair. And Dirty-Knees."

"Dirty-Knees?" she echoed, giving him a look.

"And Flashing-Eyes," he said with a smile.

"But you are Mog, and when I say Mog, it makes me think of all the things you are to me."

"All of them? In one word?"

"Yes," she said solemnly. "Especially the short-comings in your personal cleanliness." She smiled and poked at his knees. "But if Old Long-Tooth is about to jump on me, wouldn't it be useful to be able to yell, 'Hey, What's-your-name! Look out!' If you have to yell 'Hey, Pretty Fleet-of-Foot Good-with-Your-Hands Story-Teller Auburn-Hair, look out! . . .'"

"You left out 'Dirty-Knees.'"

"When I'm already swallowed by that cat, I don't think my cleanliness or lack thereof will be at all relevant."

"Well, since there's only the two of us here, I think I would just yell, 'Look out!' and hope that you would realize that I probably wasn't yelling to myself."

"It wouldn't be the strangest thing I've seen you do," she said with a look that hinted she could speak at great length on that subject if asked.

Mog didn't ask. He inquired instead, "Do you really want a name?"

"No," she said, flashing a grin. "I just wanted to be sure you weren't holding out on me. I've never had a name. It might be fun."

"You wouldn't like it," he said, very definitely. "It would be like a set of furs that never fit right, but cramped and hindered you at every turn. You'd have to stretch it and pull it and twist it to cover everything that needed covering, and by then it'd be so ragged and threadbare and you'd be so bored with it that you'd just want a new one anyway."

"Ah, you know me so well," she said, giving him a look that said he hadn't begun to scratch the surface. It changed to a thoughtful look. "Maybe I'll choose my own name, someday."

Mog nodded and smiled, but he wasn't sure he liked the idea of anyone else making up names. Not even What's-her-name.

Eventually winter melted away and warm days sprang up around them. Not-so-little Mog and the young woman were always sublimely happy together until one day he noticed he was miserable.

"I'm homesick!" he cried, which was a new word, but it took her no time at all to get the drift of it. "Let's go back and visit the old Tribe," he suggested. "It would be fun."

"You ran away from there," she reminded him. "Because you weren't appreciated."

"Well, maybe they've learned to appreciate me by now."

"And maybe they've forgotten you completely."

Mog had often imagined how much the Tribe was missing him; the notion that they might forget him so easily had never even occurred to him. It wasn't a thought he liked, and it seemed somewhat rude of her to suggest it. "Well, they'd be glad to see *you* at least," he said, to change the subject.

"Why? They never liked me."

"Never liked you? Didn't you see their faces around the fire when you told your stories?"

"Yes, but I also saw their faces at all the other times of day. When I first came to the Tribe, they wanted me to go away. And when I stayed, they tried to pretend I wasn't there. And when I told my stories, they liked them, but they still didn't like me. If they could have had the stories somehow without being stuck with me, that would have been perfect. All except Pog. She didn't know what to make of me, but she liked me for your sake."

"Then come back with me to see Pog."

"No, you go back by yourself if you must. Pog and Brog will be glad to see you, and they'll be pleased to know that you're happy with me. But the others have gotten all they can from you, and soon enough you'll remember why you had to leave, and then I'll be waiting here by the sea for you."

They had several conversations in this same vein until it became clear that neither mind was going to be changed. Finally, she put together some food for him and waved him good-bye.

His steps were slow and faltering with many a backward look, until she stopped waving and disappeared into the cave. Then, without his realizing it, even as he was thinking how sad he was, his steps became jaunty and very satisfied with themselves. A married man, even one as happily and casually married as Mog was, always thinks there's something he's been missing. He can't name it, but he knows it's just waiting for him to come along and discover it.

He went a longer way, looking for an easier climb over the bluffs, and that brought him to the beach where she had showed him the turtle shells. He re-membered the girl-woman leading him through the first great journey of their long-ago youth (a few months before), and suddenly he felt very lonely and was sure that he was making a terrible mistake. He didn't even have a name that he could call out to ease his sudden burst of loneliness. "Pretty," he tried. And "Fleet-of-Foot." And "Auburn-Hair." Those all helped somewhat, because they were nice things he had said to her and he hoped she remembered them. Then he thought, "Dirty-Knees," and that made him want to cry and go back and beg forgiveness. Seen through the filter of separation, what had been a harmless joke seemed an unforgivable insult, and he just knew that was all she would remember him for now that he had been out of her life for . . . well, about twenty whole minutes now.

He was too miserable to notice anything. He didn't notice that the only turtle shells remaining were those that were too large to carry away. And he didn't notice the many prints of many feet in the sand that even the winter storms had not entirely washed away. It was lucky there weren't any large, hungry beasts lurking about, because he wouldn't have noticed them, either, and he would have made an easy meal just then, albeit a bitter one to swallow.

He was lonely in one direction and homesick in the other, and it was only momentum that kept him moving forward. For three days he stumbled on, always just a hair away from turning right around and heading back.

When he began to see familiar landmarks, he was thrilled at first. "There's the big rock with the notch in it!" he would think with excitement. Then he'd think, "I've seen that a million times before. Who cares about a silly rock? But at least it means I'll soon get to the cave, that dear old cave that was my home for so long." And then he'd remember how dank and dark and dismal it was. And then he'd think of the cave by the sea and how delicate and delightful and delicious . . . well, it wasn't really delicious. And it wasn't very delicate or delightful either. In fact, dank and dismal pretty much summed it up, too; it was a cave, after all. But it was a cave that held *her*, so he could only think good words of it now.

He might have turned back then, even though he was almost to his goal, but he thought of Brog and Pog, and he knew that he would be happy to see them, no matter what. So he trudged on.

"Halt, who goes there?" called a voice, and suddenly Quog jumped out from behind a rock, brandishing a spear. "Ow! I got a splinter! Oh, hi, Mog. Say, I haven't seen you around lately. Where have you been?" Quog was so wrapped up in his own bodily woes that he wouldn't have missed Mog unless Mog had been a spare leg that had somehow wandered off on its own.

Mog's first feeling was disgust. What was the point of running away if the very people you were running away from didn't know you had run away? If a tree falls in the forest, does anyone know what it won't stand for?

His next feelings were surprise and curiosity. Because Quog had a couple of turtle shells hanging from a cord around his waist. "What are those?" asked Mog.

Quog laughed contemptuously. "I guess you *have* been gone if you don't even know what these are."

"Well, I know what they are, they're turtle shells. I meant why are you carrying them around?"

"'Turtle shells'? What are turtle shells? These are greenbacks, and they show how important I am. I've been paid two whole greenbacks to stand here and watch the trail."

Mog had never heard of "greenbacks," and he'd never heard of being "paid," but he didn't want to know about new words. "How long do you have to stand here for?" he asked instead.

Quog frowned. "That was never mentioned. Do you think I should have asked for three?"

"I really don't know. I'd better be getting on now."

"Well, you can't pass till you say the password."

Confused by yet another expression that he was quite sure he hadn't invented, Mog asked, "What's 'the password'?"

"The password is 'rock,'" replied Quog in a friendly sort of way. He hadn't really grasped the basic purpose of his duties yet.

"The password is 'rock,'" Mog repeated, trying to make sense of it.

"Right, off you go," said Quog, proving that he was

seriously overpaid, no matter how few the greenbacks and how long the shift.

Mog wandered on, thinking about the strange words and phrases he had heard. Words had always been a part of him before, but suddenly they had a life outside of him. They were no longer his words, they were a language, a language that he had invented, but that had slipped out of his control and had changed and grown without him. He wondered who controlled it now.

There was the little pool, just as he remembered it. Beyond it, the wide ledge with the caves opening onto it, leading upward to the open space of the great fire and the High Cliff. The Tribespeople were coming and going, washing and cooking and talking and roaming as their whims took them.

Everything was just as he remembered. With one small difference. He had no chance to feel joy at the familiarity or disappointment at the sameness. What he felt was confusion. Everything was the same, except there were turtle shells everywhere. "Greenbacks," he corrected himself, but that didn't make it any less peculiar. And they weren't lying around in the accidental configurations that death had given them or even the casual way in which Quog had worn them. No, these greenbacks were arrayed in ways that were obviously deliberate, yet totally incomprehensible.

There were greenbacks perched on people's heads and decorated with mud and feathers, like peculiar birds hatching featherbrained ideas. There were greenbacks covering both forearms up to the elbows, like a matched set of man-eating turtles chewing along at the same disarming rate. There were greenbacks shoved onto feet, their owners trying to look self-important even as they were undermined by the stumbling clip-clop of their pedestrian musical accompaniment. But most disturbing were the greenbacks that hung from earlobes, causing overbalanced heads to flop suddenly to one side or the other and making any abrupt head turns extremely dangerous for unwary bystanders within the radius of the swing.

Mog walked through this clopping, hobbling, bobbing midst, nodding and saying hello and trying not to stare at their new additions. Yet they thrust their heads and arms and feet forward in impossible contortions to be sure that Mog would see their new adornments. They even wagged their heads so their earlobes bounced and danced and stretched in a way that made Mog a little sick to his stomach.

Finally he came to his own home cave. Seeing it in all its dismal sameness cheered him a bit, and he rushed into it calling out to his parents. There were the old stalactites and stalagmites, the familiar puddles, the same soot-blackened ceiling, good old Drog, the usual . . . "Drog?" he thought.

And "Drog?" he said. "What are you doing here? Where are my parents? Where did all these greenbacks come from? Why . . ." He stopped because Drog stood up and looked at him, and Mog could scarcely believe it was really Drog.

First of all, Drog was wearing a suit. Well, not a suit. It was, after all, still furs, and there were no lapels or vents or slim-line tailoring. But what could be done with a sharp-edged stone and a bone needle had been done. Gone were the scruffy leavings he had always worn—these furs were finely dressed and carefully joined and brushed. They didn't even smell very much.

Then there was his personal appearance. His face was clean. (This made him almost unrecognizable. It was curious that the clearer you could see him, the less he looked like himself.) His hair wasn't matted; it was neatly arranged and slicked down with (sniff) aromatic bear grease?

But most of all there was his attitude. He stood and stared unblinking at Mog with no sign of fear or uncertainty or shiftiness or any of the other qualities that made up the very essence of Drog-ness. If it were not for the dent in his forehead, the reminder of many lost conversations, he would be completely unrecognizable.

"Well, young Master Mog," said Drog in a condescending drone. "So nice to have you back among us, even if you have chosen to make your appearance in a place that, while once most fitting for such an occurrence, has since undergone a change of circumstance that makes your abrupt entrance, though understandable given the limits of your knowledge, wholly inappropriate in the current situation."

Mog gaped in horror. "My words!" he would have shouted if he could have spoken. "What have you done to my words?" This was what all his words had come to, this terrible, twisting, turning, tangled snarl of clause and defect. And he suddenly suspected he knew where the greenbacks had come from, too.

"So," Drog dragged on, "while we forgive this unintended intrusion, we would suggest that you withdraw with all due haste to reconsider your—"

Mog finally regained his tongue. "Where are my parents, Drog!? And what are you doing here, Drog!? And what . . . what . . . what have you done to my words?!"

The eyes didn't falter, they didn't flinch; they burned with indignation, and the mouth was opening to release what twisted beastly words Mog couldn't even imagine, when suddenly a bent figure, face down, sidled up to Mog, grabbing his arm and urging him backward, away from the wrath of Drog.

"Forgive he," the figure said, face down. "He not understand, Mayor Drog. No be angry, he be good. Forgive all, please, Mayor Drog."

The stooped figure shuffling backward was unrecognizable, but the syntax was unmistakable. "Father?" asked Mog, hesitantly. "Brog? Drog, what is—"

The hand that clenched his arm then had all the strength of the mighty hunter, but the voice and the attitude were more Drog-like than anything in the new, improved Drog. "*Mayor* Drog!" the bowed figure corrected. "Mayor Drog!" And jerked Mog backward out of the cave.

Mog's last view in the gloom was of Drog brushing back his hair with a satisfied smile.

17

(THUMP) "MAYOR DROG"

Brog was trying to get Mog away from the cave and hug him at the same time. It was easiest finally to pick him up and carry him away, which Mog found more than a little embarrassing.

"Glad see you," Brog said fervently, even as he toted Mog away.

"Me too," said Mog, squirming out of his arms and losing a bit of grammar in the struggle. He was glad to see Brog, but his gladness was equaled by confusion and outrage and embarrassment. "Why is Drog in our cave?"

"Mayor Drog, Mayor Drog," Brog muttered, as if he must keep reminding himself. "Not our cave, *his* cave. Him buy. Give many greenbacks. Me make good sell. Good see you." He got a grip again and rushed Mog onward.

Mog sighed and gave in. "Well, at least you aren't covered with greenbacks like the others."

Brog looked hurt and a little defensive. "You no think me have greenbacks? Got plenty greenbacks. More than any except Drog himself." He stopped for a moment to shift Mog under one arm so he could hit himself three times in the head with the other fist while repeating, "Mayor Drog, Mayor Drog, Mayor Drog." Mog wondered where Brog's club was. That would normally be Brog's favored method of talking to himself.

"Plenty greenbacks," Brog repeated, looking sullen. "Just Pog don't like me carry them out where things can happen to them."

"What can happen to them?"

"Oh . . ." Brog's eyes shifted about. "Me can forget and leave them somewhere," he finally admitted. "Only do it once, but she no trust me more. So keep in pile at home where Pog can guard."

"You keep them in a pile at home?"

"*Big* pile," Brog said defensively.

And it *was* a big pile, Mog discovered, when they arrived at the new cave, which was dark and dank and dismal, just like home. This was depressing enough, but, to make it worse, there was Pog sitting on top of the big pile of greenbacks, holding a spear and trying to look threatening. Her face was a scowl, but she held the spear tip carefully elevated so no one might trip and get scratched on it. It was such an unnatural mix of savagery and kindness that Mog wanted to cry, but Brog was carrying him more or less upside down, and if his nose starting running, he might drown.

"Look who me find," Brog announced proudly, holding Mog out to his sweetly snarling wife. He smiled at Mog's feet until he realized that was the wrong way up and flipped him to bring his more recognizable features into view.

Pog was squinting too hard (to make her scary face) to see him at first. When she unsquinched her eyes enough to recognize him, she instantly threw aside her spear and slipped down from the teetering pile to grab him up in her arms. "Mog!" she cried, and "Oh, my Mog!" And this was the best part of the homecoming, and Mog cried some and wasn't at all embarrassed by it.

But, suddenly, she let him go and hissed. "Listen! Did you hear something?" She snatched up her spear and looked around for thieves. Then she saw Mog again and hugged him again and cried some more and it was still good, but he couldn't take his eyes off the pile of greenbacks over her shoulder. "No," he told himself, resolutely. "Not 'greenbacks,' 'turtle shells.'"

"Why did you leave us like that?"

"I left because no one appreciated me anymore. I did everyone a great service by inventing language, and they just used it to make fun of me."

"Too bad no greenbacks then," Brog said thoughtfully. "We could have selled every word separate and got real rich." He eyed Mog warily. "Me suppose you want some of these," he said, pointing at the pile.

"Don't be stingy," Pog said.

Brog rolled his eyes. "Oh, sure, me do all work to earn, then just hand 'em over to you and Mog. How me ever catch up with Drog—(thump!) *Mayor* Drog!— if me have to support all three of us?"

"Drog?" Mog just couldn't understand. "You're trying to be like Drog?"

Brog nodded resolutely. "Sure! Him richest man in town."

"'Rich?' 'Richest?' Where do these words come from and what do they mean?"

Brog looked confused. How could Mog not know

what a word meant? "Most greenbacks makes you richest," he said, explaining the obvious.

Mog thought that "rich" should be another word for "crazy," but he didn't say it out loud. "So what does Drog do with his riches? What good do all his 'greenbacks' do him?"

"Well," said Pog, "he owns all the food in Here."

Mog looked around the cave. "In here?"

"Not in here. In *Here*. In the whole Tribe."

Mog was stunned. "No one else has any food? Don't you hunt anymore?"

"Sure," Brog said, a little irked. "Me still best hunter. And me charge him good price for everything we kill. That's why me so rich, second only to Dro— (thump) Mayor Drog."

Mog couldn't begin to untangle all the questions he had. Pog tried to explain. "Drog disappeared at the same time you did."

"*Mayor* Drog," Brog interjected.

"Well, he wasn't mayor then," Pog replied. "That was before the election."

"Election?" Mog wondered, but he kept quiet.

"Drog—" she started again. "Soon-to-be-*Mayor* Drog—" she amended, with a look at Brog, who tried

148

to pretend he hadn't been about to correct her. "He came back with the first greenbacks and bought some food. Whenever he ran out of greenbacks, he'd disappear again for a week. Every time he returned, he had more greenbacks and he bought more of what the hunters killed and the women gathered."

Now Mog recalled the beach empty of all except footprints and the largest of the shells. He shivered as he realized that Drog had followed them down to the shore.

Pog told her story, impeded only by the occasional help from Brog. Mog was surprised to realize that, besides the story she meant to tell, he was hearing an entirely different one that she told without knowing. Words could convey meanings you didn't suspect when you put them together. It was all there if you just knew how to listen.

Pog told a story of how much good Drog had done for the Tribe, how he had saved them and been kind to them again and again. Pog and the other Tribespeople had convinced themselves that this had truly happened. But here was the story that Mog heard underneath that one:

The Tribespeople began giving Drog anything

extra they had—furs, dried food, scraping stones—in exchange for greenbacks. It was called "selling." Eventually, there was nothing to sell but the fresh meat from the hunt, which the men brought directly to Drog. The women were delighted to get the greenbacks that were their share, but when they realized they had no food for the evening meal, some questioned whether those greenbacks were so wonderful after all.

But Drog, without urging, brought out enough food for everyone from the private stock he kept in his cave. Their stomachs were filled until there was scarcely room on their laps for their stacks of greenbacks. They danced around the fire, singing the praises of life in general and Drog in particular.

It was that night that someone first hit on the idea of wearing their greenbacks. A little bit of fur, a few feathers, cram your head halfway up into the tail hole and there you had it: gaudy, extremely uncomfortable and impractical. It was an immediate hit. It was not only a display of wealth but also high fashion. Everyone vied to outdo each other in display. The more it hurt and the less protection against the elements, the higher the fashion.

That settled it. Greenbacks were here to stay.

Drog brought back more greenbacks and bought more food and still shared freely. Perhaps he never brought out quite as much food as that first night and perhaps there was a little less each time, but the Tribespeople were used to that. You couldn't expect a feast every day. Everyone was happy. They had their greenbacks and their relatively full bellies besides. At first.

The day came when Drog had no more greenbacks. Some men laughed at him (which set their greenback earrings swinging in a painfully fashionable manner). The women thought it might be a bad idea to irritate the man who provided the food even if he *was* a loser in the fashion department. But Drog took it well. He just smiled and shrugged at their jokes. Good old Drog.

Then dinnertime came. And the food didn't. But the snow did. The first flakes of snow were drifting down as the women came to Drog's cave to ask him, timidly, what there might be for dinner. (The men who had laughed made themselves as inconspicuous as was possible with turtle shells swinging from their ears.)

Drog was apologetic but, as they had so amusingly

pointed out (clanking of embarrassed heads ducking down between their shell earrings), his store of green-backs was exhausted. This meant he could buy no more food than he already had, and now that the snows had come, he had to think about himself first. The Tribespeople would just have to make do with the supplies they had. Hadn't they saved something for the coming cold?

The men laughed at that ridiculous question. The women looked nervous. The Tribe withdrew to discuss the situation. "How much do we have?" the men asked. The women were vague about the amount of food they had in storage, although they could be very precise about how many greenbacks they had. When everything was produced, they were shocked to discover that the total food stocks of the Tribe amounted to a few roots and a bit of dried meat. The men were extremely disappointed in the women, but a few good thumps on their resonant greenback hats silenced their complaints.

Roots and a bit of dried meat. That was all anyone had. Except for Drog.

They went back to Drog and offered him a green-back for a bison's worth of meat, which had been the going rate when Drog was buying. But Drog pointed out, regretfully, that soon the hunting would become impossible, so the food was worth much more now. A greenback that had once bought a whole animal would now buy only a haunch. The Tribe's stomachs were speaking louder than brains by this time, so the deal was made. The Tribespeople regularly received their smaller-than-ever ration of food, and the greenbacks began to return to their neat piles in Drog's cave.

The snows were not yet deep on the ground when Drog had all the greenbacks as well as all the remaining food. It was hard to say whether the Tribe found it more painful to be unfed or unfashionable. The Tribespeople didn't know what they could do, but kindly Drog again had an answer: he would buy their caves from them. He would pay a very good price (at least, he said it was a good price; who knew what a cave was worth?), and they could continue to live in the caves in return for a modest number of greenbacks to be paid to Drog every full moon. Everyone agreed, and for a day they were happy to deck themselves out again and see a stack of greenbacks back in the corner of their caves. (Drog's caves, actually, but they didn't think about that.) Then they paid for their food. They paid their rent. The stacks dwindled and the fashion became sparse.

When the snow was at its deepest, they had no greenbacks, no food, no stalactites over their heads they could call their own. Drog was very concerned for them. He scarcely knew what he could do, but finally he devised a system whereby they could eat now and pay later. A tough, dry haunch of meat right now would cost only two bison when the green plants returned.

It seemed a good deal, meat now for hunting later. It seemed that way right up until the snow melted. Then they found that they had to hunt all day, every day, to stock Drog's larder while they survived on half rations. Gone were the happy times of taking it easy for a few days after each big hunt. They were exhausted, their stomachs growled, and their caves weren't their own, but that wasn't the worst of it. With all that they lacked, there was one thing they still wanted more than any other in the world, more than rest, more than food, more than shelter.

Greenbacks.

Having owned them for a while, it was intolerable to be without them. They were gradually paying off their cold season debts, and they would soon (with their improved hunting skills) be able to pay their rents and still live well and even begin to lay up food for the snows to come. But this, which would once have meant perfect happiness, now meant nothing so long as their heads weren't burdened with fashion, their ears weren't sore from adornment, their feet weren't pinched by wealth. A corner of their hearts was just as empty as that corner of the cave where the greenbacks were once as high as a mastodon's eye.

How to get them back? Drog had all the food he needed for ages to come. What more did he need to buy from them?

Once again Drog (good old Drog!) came to their rescue. Out of the goodness of his heart, he found little services the Tribespeople could perform for him, and in return he paid them very well (according to Drog). The best clothes-maker completely redid his wardrobe—two greenbacks. The best washer kept his new wardrobe in top condition—one greenback. Pog, who was the best cook, prepared his meals especially (using all the secrets she had formerly lavished on Brog, who was reduced to chewing on dried meat)—three greenbacks. One man sold him the best spear in the Tribe;

another carved decorations into it. When Drog didn't feel like walking, two men carried him on a litter. When the weather got warm enough, women fanned him with palm fronds.

While the men hunted and the women gathered, Drog would sit on the bank of the little pond in his fine furs and nibble on the tidbits that Pog prepared for him. The Tribespeople came to him there at the bank and paid their accounts. (Drog told them how much they owed, and they never thought to question his accounting.) When they couldn't seem to get ahead, but were always bringing back the greenbacks they had just been paid, Drog worked out loans so they could keep their greenbacks and wear them and stack them and enjoy them, and all it cost was a little larger share of the hunt each time and a few more little services for Drog's comfort.

Then one day, Drog called everyone together and told them that they needed a Mayor. They congratulated him on this brilliant idea and thanked him for his consideration and nodded a great deal and finally fell silent. Eventually, Brog asked where they could get one of those Mayors, and could they bring it down with spears or should they dig a pit? Drog explained no hunting was involved; they would *elect* a Mayor. This led to another round of congratulations and thanks and nodding and silence. Drog eventually explained how each man would get a vote (*and* each woman—Drog was perfectly willing to be progressive as long as he knew he'd get what he wanted), and the result would be binding on the whole Tribe. They all agreed this was very fair, but they weren't sure how to proceed.

Drog cast the first vote—for Brog. Everyone was surprised, not least of all Brog himself. Brog didn't feel like a Mayor, whatever that was. He was still the best hunter, but that just meant he did most of the work to provide the food that Pog would prepare for Drog.

Shog had stepped forward to agree with Drog and cast his vote for Brog when Drog hurried to explain himself. "Yes, the Mayor should be wise and always thinking of the future and able to care for the Tribe and to express himself fluently. And Brog is . . . well, our best hunter, and I, for one, think that should count for something."

Drog clapped Brog on the back, and in spite of himself Brog felt pleased. Maybe he did deserve to be whatever Mayor was and it was good of Drog to say it. Brog didn't notice all the dubious stares he was getting, particularly on that "express himself fluently" comment.

"Me vote for me, too," Brog said proudly.

Suddenly, Shog shouted out, "I'm voting for Drog!" and there was a general roar of acclamation. Before you knew it, Drog was Mayor, no matter how much he shook his head and tried to wave it off. Finally, he said it was a terrible responsibility, but he was willing to accept it for the good of the Tribe.

So Drog was elected Mayor.

"Mayor Drog," Mog said, shaking his head.

"*Mayor* Drog," Brog corrected, out of pure habit.

"And being Mayor means . . . what, exactly?" Mog asked.

Brog opened his mouth and shut it and looked at Pog, who did the same back at him. Finally, she shrugged. "I'm not sure, exactly, but everybody has to do whatever he says."

Brog nodded happily, glad to hear such a concise definition.

"But no one likes him!" Mog exclaimed. "He's slow and clumsy and lazy." His parents nodded their agreement, waiting for him to reach his point. Mog felt flustered at stating what seemed obvious. "You never used to trust him to do anything."

Brog brightened at that, happy to clear up his son's misunderstanding. "Well, you see, him still no do anything, him just give orders. *We* do everything, so that all right." Brog was pleased to express himself so logically.

"You *do* everything and he *owns* everything."

"Why you say that? We have many greenbacks. We rich."

"But the greenbacks just represent how much you owe him. He owns the food and the caves and all your labor for a long time to come, and all you get are some turtle shells that are really his anyway."

"What 'turtle'?" Brog asked politely.

"Don't you see how ridiculous all this is?" Mog burst out in frustration. "Mayors and greenbacks and that lazy good-for-nothing owning everything and everybody working for him?"

Brog lost his smile. Pog stared at the floor. "It does seem ridiculous," she said softly, "now that you say it that way, out loud. But it didn't seem ridiculous when everyone was part of it, when the whole Tribe went along with it. It only seems ridiculous when there's someone outside talking about it, someone not part of the Tribe."

That stopped Mog cold. "Me? Not part of the Tribe?"

"Yes," Pog said, looking at him sadly. "You've been gone a long time, and the Tribe has changed while you were away. There were hard times and you weren't here to help with the hard decisions, so things have turned out as they have and you're not a part of them, and we have to make do the best we can."

"But now that I'm home, I can help change things."

Pog shook her head, gazing at him with love and sadness. "Are you home? I don't think this is your home anymore."

Mog was stunned. "You don't want me here?"

"Yes, I want you here!" Pog burst out. Her look was still loving, but it became fierce, like a hungry beast that would eat you with its eyes. She suddenly looked like the strange little girl, that first night in the firelight. "I want you more than I ever wanted any- thing. Except Brog," she added, turning and touching his chest with her fingertips. Brog wasn't sure of all that was being said, but he knew the love in her voice and he folded her into his arms.

"This is just a place for you to visit now," Pog said from within the shelter of Brog's strong arms. "This isn't your home." When Mog started to protest, she asked, "Where is the strange little girl?"

His thoughts instantly flew to her, and he wished that he could follow them. "She's . . . at home," he admitted.

"Where you home now?" Brog asked.

Mog thought of the cave by the shore and the water and the waves. But mostly he thought of her. "Wherever she is," Mog replied, realizing the truth of it. "That's my home now."

Pog nodded, full of love and sadness and acceptance. "Stay with us," she said, "as long as you want— as long as you can—as long as you will. Then go home. Lead your life and leave us to ours. We'll listen to your ideas, but don't make trouble for us and the Tribe. Stay away from Drog while you're here."

Mog shrugged. He didn't like it, but she was right. He had quit the Tribe; it was wrong to stir up trouble if he didn't intend to stay and see it through.

"All right," he said. "I'll keep my thoughts to myself. I'll even call him 'Mayor' Drog. I'll just decide that 'Mayor' means 'stupid,' and it will be a pleasure."

Brog wasn't sure about that last bit, but the rest

sounded good, so he smiled. "It not so hard, no have to see Mayor Drog much, only dinner and Morning Greeting."

"Morning Greeting?" Mog asked.

Brog blundered on, missing a warning look from Pog. "You know, all Tribe come to High Cliff in morning to greet—" He stopped abruptly.

Something was wrong, but Mog couldn't understand what it was. After a pause, he finished Brog's sentence. "The sun."

Brog made a little whimpering sound at that, but Pog put a hand on his arm and he didn't say anything, just stared up at the roof and tried to look unconcerned. He would have whistled a carefree tune if any had yet been composed.

Mog matched his nonchalance. "It didn't have a name when I left," he said. "That's why I didn't know what you meant. But now it's called the Morning Greeting?"

Brog nodded and smiled vaguely as if his thoughts were more than ninety million miles away.

"And I wouldn't be surprised," Mog went on, casually, "if one of the Mayor's duties is to stand on the High Cliff."

Brog's smile crumbled as his thoughts plummeted back into earth orbit. He nodded again, feebly.

"And no doubt," Mog went on blithely, "it is he who has the honor of actually calling out the name of the—"

"Enough about us," Pog said brightly. "Tell us where you've been and what you've done." Mog tried to finish, but Pog insisted. "Tell us about your new home and the strange little girl."

Mog talked of his adventures and his new life. But he knew there was one more thing they hadn't told him, perhaps worse than all the rest. He wasn't sure what it was, but he suspected that, come morning, it would be as plain as the big yellow you-know-what in the sky.

18

HERE AND THERE

She was out of the habit of being alone.

It was a habit she didn't regret being out of. It was Mog who had forced twoness upon her, and she didn't regret anything about him, even the really regrettable parts. No, she didn't miss being alone.

It was just that she had been so good at it, for so long. You have to love something you're so good at, even if you don't like it.

Why had she been alone so long? Mog had tried to ask, but she had avoided answering out of embarrassment.

Why had she left her parents, her tribe, everything she had known? What was her deep, dark secret? Why couldn't she tell? Was it because the answer was too terrible, too heartbreaking, too—

No, it was because it was too ordinary.

She didn't get along with her parents.

That was it. Nothing earthshaking, nothing tragic

or romantic. Let Mog imagine what he would, she was embarrassed to admit that her lonely quest had been inspired by ordinary incompatibility.

Her parents wanted her to be like everyone else, and there were times when she wanted that, too. But then the ideas would come, the imaginings, the day-dreams, the pictures glimpsed and then gone with nothing to fix them and make them real.

She tried to share them with her parents. When her mind would wander away from her chores, she would try to act out what she was seeing. Her parents would gently explain (as gently as was possible with a club) that chores were more important than playing strange games.

She tried to share them with her friends, breaking into their play to pantomime her thoughts. They showed their appreciation with stones and twigs and harsh laughter.

She tried to share them with her tribe. She stood up beside the fire one night to show them, but that was the place for the men, and she was sent to bed hungry.

She walked away from the fire, discouraged and disheartened, and she didn't stop walking when she got to her cave. She walked down the hill and out into the world.

It was a hard life, being on her own. But once she dealt with the basics of survival, she was free to explore the wonderful place that was in her mind. She told herself that she was all that she needed.

Yet no matter how strange she is, no little girl is an island. There was a need that brought her to the Tribe, that drew her to the fire. And then Mog's words came arching across the water to the island of her secret self. Suddenly, his words gave her the way to cross over to other people, not to become one of them but to share with them the world where she most truly lived. She built bridges of words, stories, to carry them to places where they could otherwise never set foot.

But the one she most wanted to visit her island stayed away. Mog refused to cross over, to be just one among the tourists. So, having already given up being just one, she gave up being one among many. She left her island to walk the shore with him. She became first one with one and then one of two. They crossed their metaphors and burned their bridges and found happiness.

Now she had acquired the habit of Mog, and that

was harder to break than the habit of being alone.

She could still get through the day. She could fish and cook and do all the things that constituted survival. She just couldn't find the joy that had once been there. The return to her island was exile rather than freedom.

Far up in their cave, where the water was a narrow brook before other springs joined to swell it into full streamhood, she knelt to stare at her reflection in a small pool.

Why should staring at herself make her think so of Mog? If she could look at him, would she think of herself? She didn't know, but she longed for the opportunity to find out.

Was he coming back? That was another thing she didn't know. She understood the pull of home and family and tribe. It had been the first thing she had had to kill so long ago when she went out alone.

Mog hadn't found his freedom when he left with her. He thought he had made his choice, but he hadn't yet. Now he had to choose, and she wasn't even there. He thought he was just visiting, but if he fell back into the rhythms of daily life, if he accepted the place they assigned him, he might just stay. Between a tribe, a whole well-established world, and one not-so-little, not-so-girlish, but still definitely strange young woman, what would he choose? Would she ever see him again?

Would she ever again hear him call her . . . Dirty-Knees?

Her image in the pool was distorted by the fall of tears, and she was disgusted with herself. She angrily wiped her eyes and watched the ripples clear from her reflection. "There I am," she told herself. "Just me, no Mog, get used to it, that may be all you ever see." She willed herself to see nothing but what was there, the auburn hair, the green eyes, the thin lips, the long fangs in the widening mouth just over her left shoulder.

If she hadn't been so busy diving straight into her reflection, she might have taken heart that she hadn't lost all her lonely skills, that she didn't hesitate a moment upon realizing that Old Long-Tooth had taken Mog's place at her side. The mighty paw that had broken many a neck in its time broke only the surface of the water, shattering all reflection as she dived a hair's breadth ahead of those splayed claws.

Long-Tooth didn't hesitate. The stream was narrow here, not like down where the two had escaped before.

Here Long-Tooth could leap across the water, and he did and was waiting when she came to the surface. But he didn't know the tricks of spear-fishing, didn't know how the light bent at the surface of the water. So he was just out of position when she caught breath and dived again.

Another leap, another miss. Back to the other side, another swipe that clawed up nothing but water. But the stream was narrowing; he had only to keep driving her up it and it would soon narrow to the point where he could reach her no matter where she broke water. It made him lazy, the prospect of another easy kill, and he hung back a moment, didn't push for that last leap.

She was out of the water in a second, up and over the little cascade at the start of the stream, into the crack in the wall that seemed only a shadow until you wormed your way into it.

The big cat thrust forward, but his big shoulders stuck fast. He could get only one paw into the cleft, and at its farthest reach it just fanned the air, like a thoughtful servant, as the young woman squeezed back into the narrowest pinch of the rocks. The water ran out between her feet, which were set on the slippery rocks to either side. She braced herself there, just out of reach.

Long-Tooth settled down to wait. She couldn't hold herself there forever. His patience was as sharp as his saber tooth and his razor claw, and it was longer and harder than those formidable weapons. He would eventually catch her on the point of his patience, and then the other two would make short work of her.

Mog woke with a start. She was in a tight spot. He had to, had to . . . No, it was a dream, just a dream. But just thinking of her made him want to be with her. What if she *were* in trouble? Of course, she would probably cope better if he *weren't* there for her to worry about. Still, he wished he was sharing whatever there was to share, good or bad, dark or bright, happy or—

Bright. He sat up on his bed of furs. He could see the cave walls around him, not yet sharp, but moving quickly from gray toward full light. It must be nearly dawn. Why had no one awakened him?

He started to rise, but Pog hurried forward from where she had been watching him. "Oh, why get up, Mog?" she cajoled, pushing him gently but firmly back among his sleeping furs. "You traveled a long way, you're tired, why not sleep a little late?"

"The Morning Greeting," he sputtered through the furs she was piling on him.

"Oh, it's probably half over by now," she said dismissively, tucking him in so firmly he was almost tied in place.

"Mother, please!" he insisted, wriggling out of both the furs and her grip. "Whatever it is you're keeping me from, I'll have to face it eventually. Better soon than late."

Pog's artificial smile faded. Sighing, she stepped out of his way.

He hurried up the trail. On the High Cliff, all the Tribe was gathered around the highest rock, just as in old days, except that the highest point was not occupied by the strength and solidity of Brog, but by the fat, slick, greasy, well-groomed lump of self-importance that was Drog.

Mog swallowed down all the bitter words that burned in his throat. He had promised to cause no trouble. Or at least to try.

"And so, fair Sun," Drog was saying in words as well oiled as his hair, "you see that your appearance and dutiful fulfillment of your obligations will be looked upon as a beneficence, albeit an expected one, and will receive all due signs of gratitude from the populace as a generality and from this administration in particular."

Mog felt sick. The words were like Drog's new appearance, nothing but the best, well chosen and groomed and put together, yet the end result was stomach-churning. Drog wanted to catch the sun in verbal tangles, to con it with contracts, to make it at best his employee, at worst his accomplice. If the sun had ears, he would do his best to hang a couple of greenbacks from them.

Where were the shouts, the threats, the club-swinging and the chest-pounding? Of course, none of that actually did any good, but it had sprung as directly from honest emotions as "Aarrgh" had sprung from many a pre-Mog throat. Was this what all his fine words had brought them to?

Brog stood near the Mayor, clearly not liking what little he understood of the syntax. He held something awkwardly in front of him, and it gave Mog a jolt to recognize Brog's old club, now strangely decorated and thrust through a greenback. Useless as a weapon, it had been made some kind of symbol. Instead of swinging it high against the dawn, Brog grasped it by the ends that protruded from the neck and tail holes and held it high in a formal pose that was both threatening and submissive. Brog hung his head when he saw Mog staring. He hadn't mentioned that he was serving Drog, that this subservient position was the reason for his second-best wealth.

Drog broke off suddenly in the middle of an offer that might have made the sun both rich and influential, and turned to Brog. "You see, Sergeant at Arms," he snapped. "The sun quite properly cannot deal with me so long as I am forced to speak from this inferior position. You will begin work today on the tower. Everyone will cease all other tasks and work on it with you. Once I am elevated to my own proper station, I will be able to speak correctly for the good of the Tribe and we will be able to establish a much more businesslike climate."

Mog couldn't stand to see Brog with his head down to Drog, taking orders, carrying his crippled club for him. It made Mog forget all his good intentions.

"The sun will never obey your orders," he called out. There were gasps, but he barreled on heedlessly.

173

"The sun doesn't accept cheap bribes; it doesn't heed fervent prayers. The sun never listened to a good man like Brog; why should it listen to you?"

He had expected anxiety from the Tribespeople at challenging Drog, but they pulled away in stark horror at his first word. No . . . his second word. He had a sudden awful suspicion that was quickly confirmed.

Drog smiled. A too-wide, too-sleek smile that beamed down upon Mog from an untouchable distance.

"Don't be frightened, good citizens of Here. This young man has erred grievously, but it is through ignorance not impiety. The law forgives without forgetting. As for his personal animosity toward ourselves, we regret it heartily but excuse it readily. Youthful passion (even when so misdirected) is to be expected and should be enjoyed when harmless and endured when otherwise. That passion will soon enough be tempered by age into the state of inaction which usually passes for wisdom. None of which excuses any further transgression once he has been removed from his natural state of ignorance. Sergeant at Arms, tell him the law and tell him the punishment."

Brog spoke quickly, without emotion and without

raising his head. "None but the Mayor shall be allowed to speak the name of the supreme object in the sky under penalty of incarceration in the jail."

Mog was shocked by the grammar before the meaning sank in. Only the utmost gravity could have forced Brog out of his natural state of original syntax.

Then he caught it. "'The name of . . .'" Brog's head snapped up and shook imploringly, stopping him just short of transgression.

"The relationship of the Tribe with the Supreme Object," Drog droned, pleased at Mog's hesitation, "is too important to be left to the casual importunings of just anyone. Therefore the wisest of the Tribespeople have decided that the name shall be voiced only by the occupant of the highest office."

"Whose name is only Drog," Mog broke in angrily. "You all have used that name in countless sentences, such as 'Where's that lazy Drog?' And 'You're as useless as Drog.' And 'You don't want to grow up to be like Drog, do you?' I used to be proud to be one of the Tribespeople; now I am glad not to be one of the Drogspeople."

"We remember how proud you were," Drog said calmly. "We remember how you walked off into the wilderness with a wild girl rather than shoulder your responsibilities as a man and a member of the Tribe."

That checked Mog's momentum. He couldn't answer that, so he avoided it. "The name you are trying to forbid me is *my* name," he said. "Well, not my name, but my word. I created it. You can't take it away from me."

Drog nodded understandingly. "That is how many of us have felt. For the good of the Tribe, we have had to give up much. But none here," (he made a wide, encompassing gesture of all his people) "has failed to make the sacrifices necessary for the good of the whole. We all hope that you can do the same so that you can take the place of honor that you rightfully deserve in the high councils of the Tribe. Will you make this great sacrifice—for your father, for your mother, for your friends—so that we can take you back to our bosom?"

Shog was quick to chime in. "It's what we all want, Mog, to have you back home."

"Join us," said a voice. "Be with us," said another.

A gentle hand was laid on his arm, and another. Mog had never felt so wanted and so welcomed. And so confused.

He had expected the People to realize he was right and rally to him. Instead they were sucking him into their own way of thinking, through kindness, through acceptance. They couldn't convince him he was wrong, but the temptation to sink into the comforting embrace of the Tribe, to play by its (faulty) rules just to have a place in the game, was almost overwhelming. He could be a member of the Tribe again. Drog would win for him the respect he had never received on his own. All he had to do was accept Drog as Mayor (whatever that was) and give up the use of one little word. This place and these people would be his home. He would be wealthy and accepted and respected.

Like Brog.

If Brog could have met his eyes, Mog could have fooled himself. But Brog couldn't look at him, couldn't wish him to become what they had become. He had never understood his son, but he honored the difference, knew it made him what he was.

Mog shook off the gently overwhelming hands and threw his arms upward. "Sun!" he cried. "Sun! I who named you now address you as the last free voice of the Tribe and command you to do exactly what you please, which is exactly what you have always done and will always do! Be yourself, Sun, and let us try to do the same!"

"Sergeant at Arms!" Drog snapped, but he saw something in Brog's eyes that he didn't want to push. "Quog! Shog! Seize him and take him at once to jail."

"I'm not afraid of you or your jail!" Mog said with a laugh, offering no resistance as they grabbed him and hurried him away. "What *is* jail?" he whispered to Quog as they descended the path.

"Oh, it's awful!" Quog replied with a shudder. "It's dark and dank and dismal. And you can never leave."

Mog shivered. He suddenly felt very alone.

On the whole, she'd have preferred to be alone.

It wasn't bad in the daylight. When the sun was up in that far-off world outside the cave, there was enough light bouncing and reflecting and skipping over the water to find its way even into the very depth of the cave. By that light, she could clearly see the long-tooth waiting patiently just outside her niche, watching her calmly, without emotion, and reaching in gently every now and then to test the distance, see if anything had changed.

The big cat was really very lovely, tawny fur stretched

over rippling muscle, deep yellow eyes set in a noble head. His great fangs kept his mouth stretched into what looked like (but definitely wasn't) a friendly, albeit well-armed, smile. She was sometimes tempted to meet him halfway, to stretch her own hand out to that great paw, to stroke the fur and pet it and make a new friend. He was as alone as she was, but he was better at it.

At night, in the dark, she knew his cat's eyes were fixed on her, drinking in the tiny bits of starlight that were too dim for her senses. It felt bad, being seen and not seeing. Still, she could hear, and what she heard was air being sucked in and out of the big lungs that powered the creature. To survive, it needed only air (which was all around) and water (which it could lap from the stream at its feet) and food. Its food was close, too, just out of reach. Eventually, she must sleep and then she would stumble forward into his embrace and find out how close a friend he could be.

In the night, in the unceasing intake and exhale of the creature, she felt what was invisible in the light: its implacable, unswerving hunger. Its appetite that could wait, it seemed, forever, but finally *would* be fed.

Oh, in the night she would have very much preferred to be alone.

But it was daylight now, and she was watching him watching her and he didn't look so bad. Strange to say, after a day and a night of leaning into the corner of her little fissure, she was tired and she was cramped but mostly she was bored. Impending disaster can only impend for so long before it becomes just plain dull. Her only hope of escape was outlasting the long-tooth, but if she died of boredom that wouldn't be much consolation.

She couldn't move more than a few inches away from the wall without bringing herself into paw range. So she flexed this foot and then that, raised one hand, then the other, always quickly because the cat was watching and each bit of exercise passed momentarily within his reach. She would raise an arm, and sometimes he would only watch and sometimes he would stretch out a paw to feel the air she had passed through, just to keep a sense of her presence. Sometimes he would guess when she was going to bring her arm back down and try to be there first. It was a sort of game, but not very interesting. It was dull as long as she won; it would only get exciting if she lost. That's not a very pleasant sort of game.

She thought about Mog. That made her lonely.

To stay awake, to stay alert, she tried making up stories and telling them to the long-tooth. She tried other ways of putting words together. She played with rhythms and sounds. He didn't like any of it at first. (It reminded him of the other talking human, the one in the shell, who was irritating even when you didn't know what he was saying.) Then, after a while, he grew to like the sound of her voice, the lilt of her phrases. He purred an accompaniment. (It wasn't a nice purr, like a fluffy kitten sitting on your lap; it was more like a small jackhammer doing road repairs under your window.) She stopped when she realized that helping the big cat enjoy the passage of time wasn't a good idea.

She tried feeling around behind her in the depths of the fissure. She found a loose rock, drew it out, looked at it. It was a rock. She thought of throwing it at the cat, but knew she couldn't get a good windup in here, so she lobbed it to him, easy, underhand. He got up, walked around it, sniffed it, licked it, pawed it. It was a rock. He shoved it aside and settled down again.

Well, that was a thrill-packed two minutes.

Another rock. Toss, lick, sniff.

Another rock. Toss, lick, sniff.

Then she struck gold. In the sense that she had an idea. There were a lot of loose rocks. The little stream-let had undercut a lot. Perhaps she could work her way deeper into the fissure. Perhaps it would open into a larger chamber. Perhaps it would lead to a way out. Moving rocks from here to there became suddenly much more interesting.

Then she struck gold. In the sense that she struck gold. She almost tossed the rock without looking, but a gleam caught her attention. The rock sparkled, threw off pinpoints of radiance, like the water in the cave. She rubbed off some dirt, found the yellow glow beneath it. She had never seen anything like it. It was lovely. She scraped at more dirt and found that the rock was soft; she could shape it with her nails.

Lovely. Interesting. Irrelevant. She tossed the rock to the cat.

More yellow rocks. One was small and round. She slipped it into a fold of her furs and kept going. If she survived, she would give it more thought then.

Long-Tooth watched and waited and pushed the rocks aside. Shiny or plain, it made no difference to him. And waited and watched.

And waited.

Quog was right: jail *was* dark, dank and dismal.

Which is to say, it was a cave.

They pushed him into the wide opening and quickly stepped back. Mog stood there looking at them, three feet away. They shook their heads sadly at him.

"I'm really sorry for you," Shog said. "If you just obeyed the law, you wouldn't be in this terrible place."

"It makes me sick to think what it must be like in there," Quog added. He peered at Mog as if watching for signs of imminent collapse.

Mog looked around the cave. It was a cave. No better and no worse than any other cave. Rocks, dirt, seepage. A cave.

"What makes this a jail?" he asked them.

Quog shook his head sadly as if this question indicated that the mental deterioration had already started. "Because you can't get out," he said carefully, not wanting to worsen Mog's creeping dementia.

Mog looked around the wide open mouth of the cave. "Why can't I get out?" he asked.

Shog, even gentler than Quog, replied, "Because it's a jail."

"It's a jail because I can't get out." Quog nodded.

"I can't get out because it's a jail." Shog nodded. Mog shook his head. "I'm not clear on this." The other two tried to look sympathetic and helpful, but it was hard dealing with the mentally unbalanced.

"If I get out of here, will you stop me and put me back, is that it?"

It was their turn to look confused. "Why would you try to get out of a place you can't get out of?" Shog wondered.

"Because it's jail."

"So you *can't* get out."

"Why not? No, don't tell me: because it's jail."

Those two happily nodding heads infuriated him. For the first time ever, he longed for a big club so he could make his argument easier to follow.

Enough talk. Actions.

Mog took two steps toward them. "I'm out," he said. "What are you going to do about it?"

Shog and Quog reacted quickly. They staggered back, let their mouths fall open in surprise and gaped at him. It wasn't a pretty sight.

Mog didn't want to cause any heart attacks. He retraced his steps. "All right, I'm in." Their expressions didn't change. He stepped forward again. "I'm out."

Stepped back. "I'm in. Out. In. Out. In." (If he had just shaken himself all about, he might have been credited with inventing the hokey-pokey.)

"Look," Mog said, walking toward them, "'Jail' is just a word. It has no special power. It's like 'sun,' just a . . ." He was talking to himself. Their paralysis had changed instantly to frenzied motion, and they were gone up the trail. He had never seen Quog and Shog move so quickly.

Mog wondered what would happen next. He took a few steps up the trail and stopped. He had no plan; he just had to wait. He didn't like waiting. He took a few steps down the trail, thought about it some more, uncertain, uncomfortable. Without thinking, he wandered back into the cave. When he realized he was inside again, he started to leave, then stopped. It didn't make any more sense to leave just because he *could* than it did *not* to leave because he supposedly couldn't.

Mog's brain hurt. So he decided not to think, just to wait for what would happen.

Because it was convenient—and for absolutely no other reason!—he waited inside the cave, which just happened to be the jail.

The girl was gone.

The pile of rocks got bigger and the girl got smaller as she slipped backward into the fissure. Finally, she tossed out a big chunk, turned her back and disappeared.

A human might have been discouraged by this, but the long-tooth knew no emotions. It knew feelings. It knew hunger, cold, heat, the satisfaction of the kill, of the full belly.

Waiting was a physical sensation, too. The heart slowed, the temperature lowered, the breathing diminished. It was a state near sleep, yet a single shot of adrenaline would fire him into action when the time came. And in near-sleep, Long-Tooth came closer to dream than he ever could in the real thing. Warm flesh, hot blood, he could almost taste them. It was very sweet to wait. He loved waiting.

As long as he could see what he was waiting for. His visions of a warm meal turned into hot air before his eyes. She was gone.

He clawed through the rocks a few times. Many of them revealed sparkles and flecks and specks and chunks of gold. He didn't care. None of them revealed any little girls.

He turned around. She hadn't slipped past some-how. He looked back. She hadn't reappeared. He pawed at the rocks. Still no girls of whatever size.

Long-Tooth would never compose a symphony; he would never build even a small cathedral; he would never design the simplest of thermonuclear devices. There were millions of things he couldn't do. But what he could do, he was very good at.

He could track (what he could follow); he could kill (what he could reach); and he could wait.

He waited.

Drog let him wait overnight. In jail. Just barely. Mog stayed close enough to the cave mouth to show he could leave whenever he chose. He just hadn't chosen yet.

When Drog finally came, he brought Quog and Shog, but left them at a distance. They were happy not to come too close.

Drog walked right in and looked around with interest, as if he'd never seen a cave before and was thinking of buying it.

"Nice place you have here," he said in a friendly tone.

"It's cozy," Mog agreed, playing casual.

"I didn't expect to find you here." Drog sat down by him like an old friend, and together they stared out into the sunlight.

Mog shrugged. "I thought I'd wait around to chat with you."

"That's nice," Drog said, nodding, smiling. "That's friendly." They sat in companionable silence for a few moments. "The amazing thing is that you invented them, but you never realized the power they had. Here you are, trapped, and all because of a single word."

"I'm not afraid of your word." Mog was losing his casualness. "Sun! sun! sun! What do you think of that?"

Drog smiled benignly. "Oh, we're alone here. You can say what you like. But that's not the word I was referring to. No, it's 'jail' that's holding you here."

Mog jumped up. "I can leave any time I want!"

"Yes," Drog agreed, jovially. "That's the truly wonderful part of it." He stood rather more slowly, threw one arm around Mog's shoulders. He used the other arm to gesture around the cave mouth. If it had only been a few thousand years later (and he'd had sleeves to demonstrate that he had nothing up them), he would have looked just like a cheesy magician.

"No physical barriers, absolutely nothing to keep you here. Except a word."

"I can leave right now, don't think I can't!"

"Of course you can. But if you do, you have to keep going. That's the power of the word."

"It's not even *my* word! It has no power over me!"

"True, it was my word. But now it's the Tribe's word. And if you're to be a part of the Tribe, you must accept its words. And if you accept its words, you must abide by their meanings."

"It's just a word," Mog grumbled.

Suddenly, Drog seemed really angry. "You're a fool, Mog! You invented the most powerful weapon in the world, and you have no idea what to do with it! That disgusting little girl had some sense of it, some idea of its power, but she used it like a toy to make them laugh and cry. It remained for me to unlock the power of the words."

"Which is?"

"Every word is a contract between the speaker and the listener. The word itself is a ridiculous thing, a breath of air blown through the lips. To think that such a thing could stand in for the thundering mammoth or the spewing volcano or the great sun itself is obviously absurd. Language is a joke, a ridiculous construction, absurdity piled upon absurdity. Unless we agree that it isn't. For language to work at all, we must agree to accept it. That makes every word a contract between the speaker and the listener. If I decide that 'tree' will mean 'rock,' then no one will understand me, and the Tribe will fall to pieces. But as long as we all agree on the meaning and agree that we will act as if talk meant something, we can build the wonderful society that you see around you.

"'Jail' is the place you can't leave. So agrees the Tribe. It's absurd, but there it is. If you leave the jail, you break the contract of the word, you deny the language, and you can no longer be a part of the Tribe."

"I left the Tribe before."

"Yes, of your own free will. This time you would be thrown out, exiled, forbidden to return."

"So the only way to be a part of the Tribe . . ."

"Is to stay cooped up in this awful little cave. Doesn't seem fair, does it? But there *is* an alternative."

Mog didn't want to ask, but the silence stretched out and he finally had to. "What's the alternative?"

Drog blinked, as if he had forgotten what they were

talking about. Then he gave an innocent smile. "Why, I could take care of you, just as I've taken care of the rest of the Tribe."

"You'd give me a job."

"I'd give you a *position*: Assistant Mayor. How does that sound?"

"What does it mean?"

Drog laughed. "Who knows? But you could be rich. You could even bring that awful little girl back if you felt it was necessary. She might even be helpful; her stories might keep everyone a little more contented while they carry out our plans."

"What would I do for this wonderful position?"

"Why, you'd be my idea man. You're bright, I've never denied that. Just not very practical. You need *me* to see the true value of your creations and put them into action.

"You'd be rich. Your parents would be secure. You'd have your little girl. You'd be happy."

"As your employee."

"As my assistant."

"It's just a word."

"So is 'jail.'" Drog gestured to the entrance and the wide open spaces beyond.

When Mog didn't walk to freedom, Drog smiled and clapped him on the back. "Two days from now, they'll have the tower finished and you shall join me for the ceremonies. It will be the beginning of a great new age for the Tribe."

Mog stared at the ground. "What's a tower?" he asked softly.

"Oh, it's sort of . . ." With a wheeze, Drog knelt and scratched in the dust. "On each side, there are two long trees leaning together like this and a platform across the top here and . . . Well, you'll find out," Drog finished, standing and dusting his hands as he caught his breath. "It will be magnificent."

"Really?"

"Of course. We will define 'magnificent' as being whatever our tower is. That's the advantage of controlling the words." He laughed heartily and moved grandly down the path with Shog and Quog falling into procession behind him.

Once Drog's face was turned away from Mog, it stopped smiling. He had not smiled so much in a long time and it hurt his face. He hated Mog, just as he hated the rest of the Tribe, even more! It was important that Mog not know that, not until his plans were complete.

If he had real power, the sort of power he was planning to have very shortly, he would have Mog executed and laugh as he died. But the Tribespeople were not yet ready to obey Drog that far. He had to be seen in his ultimate position, far above them all, the equal to the sun. Then his will would be law. Until then, he had to neutralize Mog's influence. He didn't want him in exile, where his name would be a constant reminder of the possibility of disobedience. He wanted him by his side, the Mayor's assistant, accepting his authority, subservient at last. No one else would dare to stand against him. And once the tower was up and he had ascended to his glory . . . well, Mog's next mistake would be his last.

Mog looked after Drog, trying to decide what to do. He was by nature a thinker, not a doer, but this was a crisis, and he had to do something. But what? Stop thinking and start doing! Choose!

This tower. What was it? Could he somehow use it against Drog? He looked at the marks Drog had made in the dirt, seeking an answer.

Suddenly, he was no longer in jail. Oh, if you looked in the cave, there was his body staring at the ground. But the thing inside that was really Mog was far away from jails and tribes and even from the strange little girl whom he loved. And very far away from choices and doing something.

He was thinking how Drog's marks in the dust could represent a tower. Just the way a word could.

The young woman was on the plains. The fissure had finally let her through into a larger cave that followed the streamlet up to where it branched off from the larger stream and plunged underground. She felt she couldn't be safe back at the shore while the long-tooth was near. She didn't know what might await her with the Tribe, but she felt she had nowhere else to go. Without companion, without weapons, without much hope, she crossed the plains toward the High Cliff.

Behind her, the long-tooth was on the move. He hadn't reached the end of his patience, but he had reached the limits of his memory. What was he waiting for? He stared at the rocks and couldn't remember. Then a distant whiff of antelope caught his nose, and he bounded out of the cave as if he had just stepped into it for a moment's rest. He climbed onto the bluffs where the antelope sometimes came, followed the stream where they drank, and by a little offshoot stream that ran into a cave, he caught another scent. His head snapped up. His nostrils flared. He remembered. He broke into a trot.

On the High Cliff, the Tribespeople labored to build a magnificent tower.

In his cave, which he didn't even remember was a jail (his memory was as short as a long-tooth's when his mind was too full of other things), Mog scratched in the dirt.

Two days passed.

One more sunrise and the story's done.

19

LAST WORDS

It was the most magnificent tower in the world.

Of course, it was the *only* tower in the world.

Still, it was pretty impressive under the circumstances. When was the last time you built a thirty-foot-tall tower? All right, then, don't criticize.

It was, in fact, the only building of any kind in the whole world.

This was not because the Tribe or any of the other people were lazy. (They were, but that's beside the point.) Cavemen lived in caves, and there were more than enough to go around. They could never have imagined a freestanding cave (which is all that a house amounts to, after all), and so they couldn't build it.

If you can't imagine something, you can't do it.

That's the great thing about words: it's easier to build something with words than with tools. (As long as you keep your vocabulary simple, there's no chance of straining your back.) And by sharing your words, you can build your idea in someone else's head, too. But then comes the awkward part: once you've imagined something, it's hard to settle for anything less. That's where the heavy lifting finally comes in.

The first imagining was done by Brog, of all people. It started after the Morning Greeting, several days before Mog's return and imprisonment.

(I know, I said there'd be just one more sunrise, but flashbacks don't count.)

After watching Drog try to cajole the sun out from behind a cloud, Brog said, "If this rock be higher, Drog—(thump)—Mayor Drog be closer to . . . uh, big yellow thing. Maybe it listen better."

Everyone laughed at the notion of a rock being anything but what it was. Except Drog, who was always quick to smell the possibilities in someone else's idea. "What could make a rock higher?" he mused.

Shog's talent for echoing what had just been said came in handy. "Another rock?" he suggested.

"Rocks are heavy," Quog commented, bringing it back to the personal level which dominated his outlook. "A rock fell on my foot once, and it was as heavy as . . . a rock," he finished, unable to think of anything else in the same class of heaviness. Everyone agreed with this weighty view of the two-rocks question. That would have been the end of it if Drog had had to do any labor of his own, but his readily available work force gave him a much more positive attitude. No effort seemed too great to him, since no effort was exactly what he intended to exert. Great work always seems noble when your part is carried out in the shade on the bank down by the pond.

So he had them carry over a rock and put it on top of the other rock, and (with a little help) he climbed to the top. He stood there for a while, enjoying the view. He could see the tops of everyone's heads, and they had to lean way back to look up at him. That seemed exactly as it should be.

Drog stood way up there, breathing in his own exclusive air, and thought about ordering up another rock. Suddenly, it didn't seem enough. A boost of only a couple of feet had lifted his thoughts right up among the stars.

Rocks were not enough, he knew. Poor, piddling earthbound things. Trees! Now there was an idea. Big, tall, sky-poking things! Who would settle for rocks when he could have trees!

There was a lot of grumbling at that. Trees were

not only heavy, they had a firm grip on the ground, and no one knew how to persuade them to move. Nothing was done until Mog's return convinced Drog that he must have a tower to complete his plans. Drog ordered the men down to the foothills to find trees uprooted by floods or pushed over by mammoths or knocked down by lightning. They grumbled a great deal, but the promise of greenbacks was the deciding factor.

They found some trees and groaningly hauled them up to the High Cliff. They laid them down there and stretched their aching muscles, but Drog wasn't satisfied. "On end!" he commanded. "Lying down, they're no taller than rocks." So they stood a tree on end, and it promptly did the treelike thing, which was to fall down again. They thought it curious that it was so hard to knock a tree down, but once it was down, it was almost impossible to get it up again. Apparently, it took just a taste of the horizontal life to make a tree swear off verticality forever. Quog could relate to that—he was very fond of the prone position himself and always slept like a log.

They thought the tree might be lonely for its roots, so they braced it all around with rocks to imitate roots. With enough rocks, the tree stayed up, but it was shaky. They stood up three more like that, and all four stood there trembling in a square at the cliff's edge. They looked impressive there, but no one would ever dare to climb such shaky trees.

One of the trees farther from the cliff began to lean toward it. They tried to hold it up, but couldn't. Brog could see it was going to take one of the other trees with it over the edge, so he pushed that one back to keep it from falling. The two trees crashed together, their branches locked . . . and they stayed standing. Moreover, they were less shaky than when they stood alone.

"Trees friends," Brog said with wonderment. "Help each other stand up."

Drog wasn't interested in arboreal bonding patterns. He quickly ordered the men to push all the trees together in a sort of teepee arrangement. It looked as if the trees should fall down at any moment, but they were actually solid enough for Quog to climb them (which he wouldn't have done without the threat of jail). Once he got to the top and found that he didn't topple over into the abyss, Quog began to enjoy himself, dancing and showing off for the whole Tribe. "I can see my cave from here," he reported gleefully.

"Now we're getting somewhere!" Drog exclaimed, letting the women fan him to cool his brain down from all this exhausting thought.

They laid rocks against the wooden framework, gradually building the structure up to the high point of the arches formed by the tree trunks, to make a sort of steep, hollow pyramid. They placed an irregular series of rocks on the side away from the cliff to make a rough stairs and, at the very top, they wrestled a flat rock into place to make a platform.

It stood at the edge of the precipice, high above the highest point of the High Cliff, the world's first building. It would never pass an official inspection, but for a first effort it *was* impressive.

The Tribe was very proud of its construction and couldn't wait for Mayor Drog to use it for Morning Greeting. Drog, however, put them off for another day. He said he needed time to prepare exactly the right words. Actually he was just waiting for a morning that was absolutely cloudless. He had no intention of strutting out all his pomp for a sun that wouldn't meet him halfway. This was going to complete his domination of the Tribe, and nothing as insignificant as the sun was going to get in his way.

Drog arrived before dawn at the jail to awaken Mog, only to find him sitting in the dirt and muttering to himself.

"On your feet, young Mog," Drog told him. "It's time to choose."

Mog looked up vaguely. "Choose what?" He remembered there was something he had been about to decide. Three days ago. Before he got to thinking.

"To accept perpetual exile or to live as a good, useful member of the Tribe for the rest of your life."

Oh, right. That. Mog shook his head to try to concentrate. "Be a member of the Tribe and serve you," Mog said, remembering.

"And be rich."

"I could just stay here in jail."

"You could, but this is a dreary place." Drog looked around. It was odd; there were markings all over everything, lines and curves, scratched in the dirt floor and scraped into the walls. Had Mog made them? And why?

"Oh, a place is no worse than what you make of it," Mog replied vaguely. "What will I have to do if I choose your way?"

"Climb the tower with me as my second in

command. There we'll stand, just you and I, lords of all we survey."

"'Lords,'" Mog repeated. "Another new word."

"Yes, and you'll like it. 'Lord Mog.' It has a nice ring, doesn't it?"

"'*Assistant* Lord Mog.'"

"You'll help with the incantations and with anything you think of to contribute to the ceremony."

"To make you look good."

"To make *us* look good. You'll have a share of everything."

"A smaller share."

"Which is better than *no* share." Drog was getting impatient.

Mog stared out into the dimness. "Could I bring my wife back to share with me?"

Drog snorted. "If everything a man could wish for is not enough for you, by all means bring her back. But know that she will be bound by the same laws as anyone else. If she cannot keep them—and, forgive my saying so, but she seems to me even less of a law-keeper than you—then she will be exiled. Or worse."

Those words hung between them for a moment. Then Mog rose with a sigh. "I'm finished with jail.

The sun will be up soon. Let's do it."

Drog laid a hand on his shoulder. "That's another thing. In here it doesn't matter, but once we're out there in front of the Tribe, only the Lord Mayor may speak that word you're so fond of."

"'Jail'?" Mog asked innocently.

"You know what I mean. You have not gotten where you are by being stupid." He stopped to look around the cave. "On second thought, perhaps being stupid is exactly what has gotten you here." He gave a big laugh, and Mog smiled ruefully. "The word I mean is 'sun,' and you must give it up as a symbol of acceptance of your position. It's such a small word, you'll never miss it."

"It was *my* word," Mog said a little sadly.

"Once," Drog agreed. "But no longer. Now it is necessary to the dignity of the Mayor."

"Mayor Drog." Mog nodded. "Of course."

They left the cave together. When the path narrowed, Mog started ahead, but Drog cleared his throat and gave him a meaningful look. Mog dutifully fell in behind him. It was hard for anyone of less than Drog's bulk to equal his slow and stately pace, but Mog gradually accustomed himself to it. Perhaps time could accustom him to anything.

The Tribe was gathered at the cliff's edge on either side of the tower. They made curious silhouettes, bedecked as they were in all their greenback finery for this historic moment. (The very first historic moment. Up until now, there had been no such thing as history; that would all change this morning.) They weren't sure what was going to happen. Would Drog take a swing at the—uh, big yellow thing? Perhaps the additional height would help him get a grip on it to wrestle it into submission. Some rudely suggested the dignified Mayor would be more successful if he just sat on it, but others feared the Mayor's considerable girth would push matters beyond mere solar intimidation and into the realm of permanent damage.

No, it had to be talking rather than wrestling. The Tribe had on many occasions listened, breathless with admiration, as Mayor Drog submerged them for minutes at a time beneath a flow of discourse that never let them break the surface for even a gasp of intelligibility. If anyone could stupefy the big yellow thing through sheer verbal assault, it was definitely the Mayor.

A buzz ran through the Tribe as they saw the two

figures approaching in the gloom. Mog had been consigned to jail; now here he was marching along beside the Mayor. What did it mean? What could happen? What couldn't? Execution? Blasphemy? Revolution? Everything was possible in the brisk air of this early morning on the brink of history and the High Cliff.

Brog and Pog were feeling emotions both strong and confused. They had suffered for Mog, trapped in the solitude of his jail. They had visited him secretly, only to find him distracted, scratching in the dirt like a crazy person. Now here he came, marching beside the Mayor like an honored assistant. Had he come to his senses? Or lost them completely?

Mog's first view of the tower was impressive, silhouetted high against the first grayness of the morning. The outlines of the little people to either side just emphasized how mighty it was. Then they got closer and Mog could see what a ramshackle affair it really was, tree leaning against tree and rocks piled over all. His steps slowed, giving Drog a larger margin of dignity, but the Mayor stopped, bowing slightly, and gestured Mog ahead of him on the stairs. He clearly preferred self-preservation to honor.

Mog started upward on the uneven stones, then

hesitated. Deep down, he could hear the rocks grinding against each other, and the high counterpoint of creaking wood striving to bear the burden. It was not a happy song.

"Go on, now, young Mog," Drog whispered, prodding him from behind. "This is your chance to show your courage and your good will, to be reconciled with the Tribe. You shall stand upon the highest place but one, just below me, and together we shall strike a bargain with the sun. I think we can agree that's worth a bit of risk?"

"I notice that I'm the one taking the risk first," Mog observed.

Drog laughed and looked around so that all could see how fond he was of Mog. "Hateful boy," he thought to himself. "Once you've served my purpose, how pleasant it will be to . . ." His smile grew wider and he laughed again, clapping Mog on the back and shoving him forward.

Mog stumbled, then climbed carefully but quickly to the high platform. Drog followed at a much slower, more stately gait. He seemed lost in thought, as if concentrating on the state of the world and preparing to speak for the good of the Tribe. Actually, he was concentrating on the state of the tower and preparing to bolt like a bunny at the first hint of imminent collapse.

Faster and slower, both reached the top.

Drog stood gravely, eyeing the backlit peaks at the edge of the horizon. The first sliver of yellow appeared. Tensed in readiness, he waited a moment longer before throwing up his hands and crying, "Sun! Reveal yourself!" The Tribespeople gasped in astonishment and knelt in awe. Mog looked quizzically at the Mayor. Without losing his stately pose, Drog showed a tiny smile and whispered, "One of the advantages of dwelling on such heights is seeing things an instant before those below."

Mog nodded. "So they think it rose at your command. Impressive."

Drog managed to look smugly modest. "It's all a matter of timing." (This was truly a historic moment, marking as it did the simultaneous births of religion and show business.)

Drog moved his arms in slow, stately gestures to conduct the sun in its rising. To Mog, he was just a fat man waving his arms, but to the watchers far below, he was impressive, in control, awe-inspiring. When your head's bent back at an uncomfortable angle, it's easy to mistake higher for superior.

"What do we do now?" Mog asked.

Without losing control of the sun for a moment, Drog whispered, "Now we call it over and have a heart-to-heart chat. It's going to reveal that it will only deal with me in the future—with you as my assistant—and that the Tribe must obey us in everything or it will cease to show its face to us."

"That's an awful lot for it to blurt out after being quiet for so long." Mog shook his head in mock wonderment.

Drog's smile became even thinner and sneakier. "It does not speak for mortal ears to hear. It will speak only through the chosen instrument."

"Or the assistant instrument," Mog suggested.

"Perhaps," Drog whispered. "I thought of a new word: 'King.' Do you think it suits me?"

"What happened to 'Lord?'"

"Now that I'm up here, it seems too small. You can have it, if you like. To take the place of the word you've lost."

Suddenly, he threw his arms wide, embracing the dawn and displaying just how far from small he had become. "Sun!" he boomed out. "Free yourself from the mountains of slumber! Arise and put on your brightest garments!" The sun was above the horizon now, growing brighter as it rose. It happened every day when the clouds didn't interfere, yet it seemed to all watching that Drog was in charge, that the sun was doing his bidding. When people are in a mood to be fooled, it doesn't take a genius to grant their wish.

"Arise! Shine!" Drog continued with appropriate gestures while the sun obeyed every order.

Suddenly, Mog called out, "Shine! Arise!" and did some hand-waving of his own. Drog shot him a sharp glance, but Mog smiled back disarmingly. "Just assisting," he whispered.

Drog nodded ponderously. "Very good. Not terribly original, but the effort is to be commended."

"I'm learning from the master," Mog said.

Drog pondered that too-sincere smile, then decided it didn't make any difference if he meant it or not. Mog could do nothing to stop him now.

Drog called in a deep bellow, "Advance and heed well our words!"

"Heed well!" Mog echoed.

The Tribespeople looked around nervously as if

fearing thunderbolts out of the blue sky. They had always thought Drog a coward, but here he was giving orders to the big yellow thing itself! No one had ever shown such courage! Of course, Brog had hurled not just orders but outright threats, but this was different, because the big yellow thing WAS OBEYING DROG'S COMMANDS! His orders coincided conveniently with what the sun always did (rise, shine, get brighter, seem to advance), but that didn't change the fact that the sun was doing exactly what he said. It wasn't going down or dimming or shooting off in some other direction. No one could doubt that it was paying attention to the Mayor and his commands. At least no one could prove that it wasn't.

Having riveted the attention of sun and Tribespeople alike, Drog spoke more quietly, but still authoritatively. "We understand that you have been confused in the past by the welter of voices, the mixture of threats and entreaties. From now on the Tribe will speak with one voice. . . ."

"One voice," Mog repeated.

"Sounds like two to me," Quog commented, his self-involvement being even greater than his awe, but a few good thumps helped focus his attention.

"One voice," Drog reiterated, "from its new height. We will pay you the respect you deserve, but only if you accept our guidance. This, then, is the voice you will heed, the voice of Drog, a humble man, yet one exalted by the election of the Tribe. You will heed only the voice of Mayor Drog . . ."

"Only Mayor Drog!" Mog cried out. Then he gave Drog a look with as much greed in it as he could muster. "Or . . ."

Drog smiled to see an emotion he could understand. He gave Mog back a secret wink. ". . . Or that of his helper, Mog. Lord Mog." A buzz ran through the Tribe at that. Lord Mog! There wasn't a man there who wouldn't give all his greenbacks—that is, most of them—well, several of them, at least—to be a Lord. Whatever that was.

"Arise, shine," Drog went on, soothingly, and "Shine, arise," Mog explained, just in case there was any question. And darned if that wasn't what the sun did, exactly as ordered: arise, shine; shine, arise; it was following orders, whether they were given forward or backward.

Drog folded his arms to show he was getting down to business now. Mog tried to match his seriousness,

2I2

although he could never equal his gravity.

"You will work today," Drog intoned. "You will send down light and warmth and proceed in an orderly path across the sky. Tomorrow, you will meet us here again upon the high tower, and your orders for the day will be issued at that time.

"And now, Sun," Drog went on in a more kindly voice, "you may make your requests of us."

He lowered his chins to his chest and seemed to listen intently. The Tribe listened too, but heard nothing. Mog, knowing there was nothing to hear, occupied his time by enjoying the gradual illumination of the wide plains far below them. He thought of what lay beyond the plains and mountains. Of who was there. He wondered what she would do in his place. He wondered what *he* was going to do in his place. What could he do? If he denounced Drog, the people wouldn't listen. Should he just accept his new position?

"Yes, I see," Drog murmured, loud enough to be overheard by the entire Tribe, which listened even harder but still heard nothing. "Thank you, my brother, we shall."

He turned his back to the cliff and gestured all the Tribe to the foot of the stairs. "My people," he called, "come closer together, just here, so that I may address my family." And so that his new friend the sun would be at his back and in their eyes, dazzling them with its (and his) brilliance.

"The sun has been most understanding—"

"Not to mention soft-spoken," muttered Quog, who could only focus so long.

"—and has asked for little in return. Some tributes of food and furs, which I am asked to select and administer for him. He is pleased that we have finally greeted him in a manner worthy of his station and has agreed to bind himself to our demands so long as they are presented to him respectfully by a person of proper authority. He recognizes the superiority of the Tribe to all other peoples on earth and is willing to be bound to whomever you select to meet with him. What was that, Quog?"

Quog looked guilty. "I said, 'We'd better choose someone with good ears.' I mean, I don't doubt the big yellow thing was talking to you, I just didn't hear anything. I guess I can't be Mayor, huh?" He smiled weakly, staring up into the dazzle. Everyone pulled away from him, just in case the big yellow thing didn't have a sense of humor.

Drog was silent for a long nerve-wracking moment. Then he laughed. Just a little. "Ah, Quog, very amusing. Of course, the sun speaks only to he who is entitled to call him by name. If you were Mayor, the sun would speak to you. Theoretically. Or if you were the Mayor's assistant. Right, Lord Mog?"

"What?" asked Mog, who had been listening to voices of his own.

Drog gave him a sharp glance. "Even though you may not speak his name, I believe you heard the voice of the sun just now. Did you not?"

Mog looked at Drog perched there in all his glory.

Suddenly, he knew he could make only one choice. He had thought and talked and dawdled and dreamed for too long. Time to start doing.

"Yes," he agreed, "as the humble and faithful assistant to the Lord High Mayor I was honored to hear the voice of the . . . supreme being as it spoke to his exalted ears. And I can tell you that . . . Mayor Drog has not told you the truth of it!"

There was a gasp from the crowd, and Drog spun around to face him. That wasn't a good idea. I won't go into the physics of it all (mass and inertia and centrifugal force and such), but the vast majority of accepted scientific theory states unequivocally that large blobby things shouldn't go spinning around on small, high platforms if they want to avoid long trips. If Mog hadn't put up a steadying hand, Drog might have found himself rudely (even fatally) demoted from his high position.

Mog gestured to the crowd with the arm that wasn't full of Drog. "The Mayor has not told you truly what was said to us by the big yellow thing." Drog would have cut him off if his full attention hadn't been on maintaining his balance.

"The Mayor did this," Mog went on, "out of modesty."

"Huh?" Drog said, in a very un-Mayorlike squeak of surprise.

Mog ignored him. "The big yellow thing didn't say it would deal only with the Mayor, it said it would deal only with *Drog*! It knows that the Tribe owes everything to Mayor Drog." A smile crept over Drog's face as he saw the openmouthed Tribe swallowing this whole. "It knows that he has brought order out of chaos, and it wishes to submit itself to the same order. It recognizes a superior being!"

"Not too much!" Drog whispered. "It's good,

it's very good, but be careful."

"I've heard it's all in the timing," Mog whispered back.

Heaving Drog to full upright position, Mog turned to face the sun and waved his arms in great swooping circles. "Get up, sleepyhead!" he called. "Mayor Drog has given his orders; now get to it!"

Drog tried to look properly modest.

"From now on," Mog continued, giving a few flourishes, "you will arise punctually and appear here before Mayor Drog on the high tower to receive your orders for the day."

"Thank you, Mog," Drog tried to break in, softly. "I'll handle this now."

"Rest your voice, O Lord High Mayor," Mog yelled back. "No need to wear yourself out dealing with servants, even if they are big and yellow." A few waves to get the sun's full attention again. "Hey! You! Don't let your mind wander. Where were we? Oh, yes, be here at dawn to get your orders. No, earlier than that! Be here at half an hour before dawn so you can get all that rising and shining out of the way and not waste the time of Drog the mighty, Drog the magnificent, Lord King Mayor Drog!"

"That's enough, Lord Mog!" Drog rumbled, trying to keep his voice smooth while his eyes stabbed at Mog's. "Do not let your zeal outstrip your respect for our honored ally. I shall speak for myself. And, of course, for the Tribe." Before Mog could say anything else, Drog threw his arms wide, giving the sun a metaphorical embrace and Mog a literal punch in the face. The Tribe gasped as Mog dropped to his knees on the edge of the abyss.

"Sun!" Drog called out in his deepest voice yet, trying to get the Tribe's attention back where it belonged. The sun was higher now, and he was momentarily blinded by a direct look at its brilliance.

"Pay attention!" Startled, Drog snapped his head around toward Mog's shout, stumbled, caught himself. The voice yelled suddenly from his other side, "Mayor Drog is speaking! Lord Mayor Drog!" The voice kept moving, circling around him.

Drog turned, trying to follow the voice. This was a mistake. There is a reason why elephants don't do pirouettes on the head of a pin. Drog staggered. There was a gasp from the Tribespeople below, part concern that the Mayor might fall, part fear that they might be occupying the spot where he would land.

"Don't be afraid," Mog assured them, squatting comfortably on the top step as the Mayor spun above him like an overweight lighthouse. "Mayor Drog has it all under control." He gestured confidently toward the Mayor, whose arms were extended, not in solar embrace, but in an attempt to balance on a platform that seemed much smaller than it had when down on solid ground. He stretched an arm toward Mog to steady himself, but Mog maintained a respectful distance.

Drog sank to his knees and planted his hands firmly on the rock. When that didn't stop the spinning in his head, he lowered himself flat on the platform and hugged it with as much body surface as he could sag against it.

The Tribe buzzed at the sight of the Lord Mayor simultaneously exalted and laid low. Mog was singing his praises, but Drog just looked fat and ridiculous and . . . well, Droglike. Mog ignored them, standing over the wreckage of Drog to continue his exhortation.

"Behold Mayor Drog," he told the sun. "Your new lord, your King! Bow down before his power! From now on, you will do his bidding, King Lord Mayor Drog! And his bidding is that you arise and shine. In other words—" Mog dropped his arms and sat, leaning back comfortably against the soft squishiness of the Mayor as he smiled at the confused faces turned up to him. "In other words," he finished, "the sun will do exactly what it was going to do anyway before anyone tried to influence it with sticks and stones."

There was a gasp at that word. Mog shrugged. "That's right. The *sun* is doing what it always did best, rising and shining; and Drog is doing what he always did best . . ." He glanced back at the Mayor's recumbent majesty. "Protecting his position by keeping a low profile."

There were no laughs. There was not even any breathing. They were all still hearing that word, that forbidden word that Mog had used so casually.

"Lord High Mog," Shog breathed carefully.

"No more Lord than you," Mog said easily. "And high only in elevation. Call me Mog; it's my name." He pointed at the sun. "And *its* name . . ." The Tribe winced.

Mog shook his head sadly. "Its name is sun," he finished.

"Please," Shog started.

"Sun, sun, sun," Mog said.

Suddenly, Brog moved two steps up the stairs, holding before him his unwieldy club of office with its greenback ornament. "Don't," he said. "No more say name."

Mog had felt calm and in control, but facing his father he suddenly became just a little boy again. "Why not? It's my word. I can use it if I want."

Brog collected his thoughts, some of which must have wandered a good ways off. "If me kill antelope, it mine, use as me want. If me give it Tribe, it belong Tribe, Tribe use how it want. You give words, they not yours no more. Tribe must decide."

"But why should the Tribe decide to give my word to . . . to this." He jerked an elbow back into the spongy mass of the Lord Mayor.

"Not give him *for* him," Brog said, slowly. "Give him for Tribe. Word still Tribe's, not his."

"Well, he's taken it for his own, along with everything else in the Tribe, so I'll just take this one thing back for myself. Nothing and no one can keep me from saying—"

"If he says it one more time, Sergeant at Arms, seize him for execution. There will be no more mercy for the blasphemer." The words rumbled through Mog like an earthquake and shook the Tribe back a step.

Mog spun to face the slitty little eyes that peered up at him. Drog had regained his breath and his poise, and he spoke with an authority that was surprising from someone who looked like a whale beached on a mountaintop.

"Give up, Drog!" Mog snapped. "You're down! They've seen you for what you are! Give up!"

Drog stared back calmly until Mog felt the silence. He turned to regard the lowered eyes of the Tribespeople. "Look at him!" he called to them. "Here lies your Lord High King Mayor Drog!" Mog laughed, but he laughed alone. No other eye met his. His laughter faltered and stopped.

Drog smiled to see the very moment when Mog realized he had lost.

"They've seen you reduced to the poor, crawling thing you really are," Mog said in wonder. "Why do they still fear you?"

"I have been reduced only to the man I always was, the man they always knew me to be," Drog replied calmly, yet loudly enough to be heard below. "If I was ever any greater, it was only because they made me so. And if they still choose me, I am still that thing, even prone here beneath your feet. You may trample me, but you will never trample the will of the Tribe."

Mog shook his head in admiration. "You use my words so beautifully. And to such hideous effect."

Mog turned to face the abyss and raised his arms, sincerely, toward the warmth streaming down upon him. "The Tribe must make its own choice. I will make mine. Whatever the consequence, I will use my words and I will speak my mind freely. And I will do it happily, even though it bring death. I raise hands and voice with gratitude to the—"

"No say word!" shouted Brog.

"Do what you must do," Mog called down to him. "I love you and I forgive you. Give my farewell to . . ." He hesitated a moment. "Never mind. I can't say good-bye to one with no name." His arms, which had faltered for a moment, stretched upward again. "You were my first word and my favorite, even though it now appears you'll be my last. I raise my voice with gratitude to the—"

Drog smiled. Brog flinched. Pog wept. The Tribe was frightened.

Mog spoke the beginning of his end. "S-s-u-u—" he got out before another voice grabbed his word and finished it differently.

"Sometimes," said that little voice that was strangely familiar and familiarly strange.

Mog smiled. Drog flinched. Pog wept. The Tribe was confused.

"Sometimes cool and sometimes hot," she said. Mog turned and started down to her, but she climbed the steps quickly past him. "I can't leave you alone for a minute," she whispered with a smile, sidestepping his attempted embrace.

At the height of the tower, she gave only a glance at Drog, who did his best to ignore her, then raised her arms to the sun as Mog had done.

"Sometimes cool and sometimes hot," she repeated.
"Sometimes shining, sometimes not;
Sometimes yellow, sometimes red,
Always just above my head."

She turned back to face the Tribe, which listened uncertainly.

"What was that?" Quog asked the strange little girl (which was how everyone would always think of her, even if she were eight feet tall).

She shrugged to show she had no idea, then looked

224

at Mog. He cocked his head and thought a moment. "I think it's poetry." She nodded. That sounded about right.

"Poetry, yes, it's poetry," the Tribespeople murmured to each other, as if they had suspected as much.

"But *why* is it?" Quog asked. "What does it do?"

She shrugged again. "It's a different way of saying something. If I can't use one word because it's been swallowed whole by a certain greedy sloth—oh, hello, Drog," she said, as if she'd just noticed him there, lounging behind her shins. "Then I'll find another way to say it. If a cave bear attacked, Quog wouldn't waste time complaining that Shog had borrowed his club; he'd just pick up a rock and use that instead."

Quog looked accusingly at Shog, who opened his empty hands to show he didn't have Quog's club. Then they looked back at the girl, who had apparently increased in strangeness even as she decreased in littleness.

"I don't mean that Shog really borrowed your club," she said, with a sigh. "That was just an example. A club is a tool and when you don't have one tool, you can always use another. A word is a tool, too, and when one word is unavailable, you only have to find another

225

that will do just as well. Mog taught me that there are many names for everything. Some nicer than others," she added, muttering "Dirty-Knees, indeed," out of the corner of her mouth. Mog tried to look apologetic, but he was smiling too broadly to make it work.

"If, for whatever reason," she went on, "you can't say the name of the big yellow thing, there are plenty of other words and phrases that will do even better. I always thought it was a boring sort of name."

Quog was still annoyed that Shog had borrowed his club, even if he hadn't. Now he spoke angrily to him. "What are you nodding about? You don't know any other words for the big yellow thing."

Shog stopped nodding and frowned in thought. Then he beamed and said, "The large, sometimes-red thing!"

"That's the idea!" encouraged the girl. "Not great, but a good first effort. How about 'Light-Giver'? Or 'Sleeper-Behind-the-Mountains'?"

Shog thought even harder, then shouted out happily. "Or Lazy-Stay-Behind-the-Clouds!" When he realized that was probably an insult, he added quickly, "But-Only-Sometimes! And-I'm-Not-Complaining!"

"Hot-on-My-Head," Quog put in, not wanting to

be outdone. "And Bright-in-My-Eyes!"

The whole Tribe began to make suggestions in excited voices. Mog and the girl beamed down happily at them.

"Fools!" Drog shouted, so suddenly and unexpectedly that the girl staggered down a step and caught hold of Mog's arm. Drog drew himself up to a seated position.

"Fools! Do you think the sun can be tricked by word games? He has forbidden you his name and you will not placate his wrath by means of this 'poetry.' These names that please you so much are as ugly as they are awkward. What name could ever please the sun so much as his own?"

The eyes of the Tribespeople dropped before the glare of Drog, with the sun itself backing him up. "Sergeant at Arms!" he called, and pointed at Mog and the girl just below him. When Mog tried to speak, Drog's voice overrode his. "In the beginning was the word! You were the first to speak the name of the sun. Everything we have today is based on that word! Now you would deny the power of the word and say that any old word is as good as another. Well, tell me what name is better than the name of the sun. Speak

227

it now, or prepare to suffer the punishment for your blasphemy!"

Mog tried to answer but couldn't. Words failed him, his own words.

Brog climbed slowly, head down, toward his son. In his hands were the club and the greenback which were the symbols of his duty.

"I'm sorry, Father," Mog whispered, but Brog did not stop to hear. He moved past Mog and the girl to the top step. He raised his eyes to Drog's, stared calmly and thoughtfully into them.

"Cloud-Hunter-Through-Plains-of-Sky," he said.

There was a long silence then as Drog stared in disbelief. "That good name for big yellow thing," Brog explained. "Cloud-Hunter-Through-Plains-of-Sky." The Tribespeople all drank deeply of the words, tasting them in their own ways.

They were good.

Brog looked shyly at Mog. Mog nodded proudly. "Now, that's what I call poetry!" he said.

Brog faced the people and spread his arms. "Waker-of-Dawn!" he called, and "Eye-of-Heaven." The people began to buzz with excitement. "Slayer-of-Darkness in dubious battle on plains of heaven," he proclaimed, and "Warrior-of-Light in struggle with night!" Brog looked surprised at that, then pleased; then he tried again. "Light so bright put night to flight. From greatest height!"

"You have it right," Mog said, clapping him on the back and laughing.

"What this called?" Brog asked excitedly. "Light, bright, night."

Mog thought. "It's a rhyme."

Brog beamed. "Rhyme," he repeated. "Poetry. Me like!"

"So do me," replied Mog happily.

Pog hurried up to take both her men into an embrace. Then she reached out and drew the girl into the circle. The Tribe gave a great cheer at the sight.

For the first time in years, Mog was completely at peace, reunited with his tribe and his wife and his family. His father was finally proud of him and his words. Nothing but happiness lay before him.

Behind him, there was still Drog.

The Lord Mayor was ignoring all the poetry and shouting. He was staring up at something. Then he was tapping Mog's shoulder. Mog pulled away, ready to strike back, but the touch was gentle. "Excuse me,"

Drog said. "Could you let me pass, please?" His voice was soft and resigned, nothing like the trumpet that had blasted Mog only moments before. "Oh, you can do what you want, but the stairs are narrow and I don't want to await the end here on this tower, so I have to ask you to let me pass. Please."

That "please" made Mog's triumph complete, and he might have done some gloating, but the young woman broke in first. "'Await the end,'" she repeated. "The end of what?"

Drog blinked. "Why, the end of the world, of course."

When that met with blank stares, Drog went on with quiet bitterness. "I hope your poetry will warm you when the final 'struggle with night' ends in defeat, and the world turns black."

Mog drew back a little. Had Drog gone mad?

Suddenly, Drog burst out angrily. "Even now you are blind to what you have done! Behold the 'Eye of Heaven' before it closes forever!" He threw one hand straight up and all eyes followed it.

The sun was half gone. Blackness had eaten it away, was advancing even as they gazed.

The people gasped. Or it might have been the sigh of the wind here on the High Cliff. Whichever, it was the only sound in the world.

Drog struggled to keep the laughter from bubbling up in him, from overflowing and filling that terrible silence. "You believed you could beat me with *poetry*?" he thought to himself. "The sun itself is on my side! I don't know if it's the end of the world or not, but I'll make sure it's the end of *you*, young Mog!"

Drog held his tongue, waiting for the Tribe to do his work for him.

Quog stuttered in terror. "The su—I mean, the big yellow thing is going out!" cried Quog.

"Something is eating the big yellow thing!" cried Shog.

"I think," suggested Pog, "it might just be the moon passing between the earth and the big yellow thing." The Tribespeople glared angrily at her for making a joke at such a serious moment.

"What should we do?"

"What *can* we do?"

All eyes turned to Drog, silhouetted against the narrowing crescent of the sun. He remained silent.

231

"What can we do, Mayor Drog?"

Drog looked surprised. "I thought Mog was your new leader."

"What can we do, Lord Mog?" asked Quog.

"There's nothing *to* do," said Mog. "Whatever it is, whether it's the shadow of the moon or the end of the world, all we can do is wait for it to finish. I'm sure everything will be fine." He smiled reassuringly. They didn't smile back.

"What can we do, Lord High Mayor Drog?" shouted Shog and Quog and half of the Tribe in unison.

"I think you know what my advice would be," Drog rumbled. "The Tribe has acted blindly, has offended the giver of life for the sake of foolish word games. Only blood can pay for the guilt of the Tribe." He gave a long, meaningful look, first at Mog, then at the sliver of sun remaining overhead. Then, most ominously of all, at Brog and his club of office.

Brog looked unhappily at Mog, who shrugged. "You have no choice," Mog said. "You must do what the Tribe wishes, and that wish is clear. Take care of . . ." He looked at her, his wife, his joy. "I wish you had a name so I could say good-bye." She started to speak, but Mog shook his head. "My words have brought me here, and I must take the last step with them." He kissed her. Brog took her hand and led her and Pog down the steps of the tower. Mog watched her go. At least he had gotten to see her one last time.

"Will you do this easily," Drog asked when they were alone at the top of the tower, "or must Quog and Shog assist you?"

Mog didn't speak. One last gaze at the girl, the woman, his other self; then he turned and squeezed past Drog to look out over the plains far below. He raised his eyes to the sun. The last sliver winked out. He didn't know how he could be responsible for this, but maybe Drog was right. Not likely, but just possible. At least Mog wouldn't have to listen to the Tribe's complaints when his sacrifice didn't work.

"See, o sun," Drog intoned solemnly, "the depth of our atonement and accept as a sacrifice the very best of us all."

"Why, thank you, Drog, that's the nicest—" He broke off when he felt Drog's hand on his back. It increased its pressure, urging him forward toward that long first step.

The sun was gone. A black disk, suddenly surrounded by a ring of gold. The silence of twilight fell

233

upon the land. Birdsong, which had gone unnoticed in the dawning light, abruptly died and screamed by its absence.

It was no ordinary twilight. The people felt a chill far beyond lack of warmth. The half-light looked brownish. Strange waves, lighter and darker, crawled in bands over everything. Mog thought of the ripples of light in the cave by the sea. It was a good thought on which to die.

Drog pushed him past the point of balance. Eyes lifted to the black hole that had been the sun, Mog relaxed and accepted his fall.

He leaned into the abyss.

Pog turned her head and screamed. Brog reached to comfort her, but she pulled away and shoved the girl to the ground.

Long-Tooth sailed over her head, just missing his pounce. He struck the stairs with all the force of his massive body. The tower shuddered and trembled. The top platform jolted forward.

Fighting for balance, Drog grabbed the only thing within reach, which happened to be Mog. The two tottered together on the edge.

Long-Tooth twisted to get his feet under him for

another pounce. The rocks of the stairs rolled and scattered in every direction. He couldn't get his footing. And the light was wrong. It made him want to sleep, but it was too soon for sleep. And why was he so far from home and chasing this little mouthful, anyway? Everything was wrong. The best thing to do was . . . eat the girl quickly and go.

She was running. He leaped for her, pushing off hard against the crumbling rock facade. The tower creaked, the platform bounced. Mog fell back. Drog fell forward. Over the edge.

Mog grabbed a handful of Drog's fur and leaned back. He dug his heels in as Drog's weight pulled him to the edge of the platform.

The girl ducked. The long-tooth missed again, but spun and pinned her to the ground with one paw. He raised his head, bared the great fangs for the killing blow.

Brog instinctively raised his club, but, stuck through the greenback as it was, it was useless.

A blinding sliver of sunlight appeared on one side of the black disk, dazzling the upturned eyes of the long-tooth, freezing him for a moment.

Brog swung the ineffectual club of office with all

his might. The greenback flew off the end of it and smashed against the long-tooth's skull. The beast staggered, and the girl was up again and running. With a shake of his head, Long-Tooth pursued while Brog followed close behind.

Realizing they were being ignored by the long-tooth, the Tribespeople looked around dazedly. Quog was the first to notice. "The sun has returned!" he cried. "I mean the big yellow thing." The people looked up.

"Mog was right," said Shog. "The big yellow . . . the *SUN* is back!"

"Mog was right, the sun is back!" the people shouted. "Sun!" and "Sun!" they shouted, loving the taste of the word. "Hooray for Mog!"

"Help!" Mog answered. The rocks had fallen in a heap around the bare tree trunks, which twisted together as the platform tipped slowly forward at the top. Mog hooked an arm under Drog's chin and grabbed the far edge of the platform as it tilted inexorably toward the vertical.

"Brog!" shouted Pog. "Mog will fall!"

Brog gave up on catching the long-tooth and raced back to the tower, but there was no way to climb it.

Quickly, he scrambled over the fallen stones to slide between the tree trunks. Bracing his club against them, he pushed with all his strength. For a moment the leaning stopped. Pog gasped. If the tower fell, Brog would be crushed beneath it, yet he was Mog's only hope. Husband and son, how could she bear the loss of either? Or both?

"Let him drop, Mog!" yelled Shog.

"Who needs Drog?" Quog yelled. "He was going to kill you!"

"*You* were going to let him," Mog called back through gritted teeth.

Shog nodded. "He's got a point there."

"I don't think we can do anything to help you," Quog called.

"Don't worry about me," Mog answered. "Help her!"

"Who?" Quog asked.

"'Whom,'" Shog put in, hoping to impress Mog just in case he survived.

"The girl!" Mog shouted.

"What girl?" asked Quog.

At that moment, the girl raced past, just ahead of the long-tooth.

"Oh, her," said Quog, who was willing to help out if it didn't involve too much danger. He was carrying no weapons, so he took a greenback off his foot and threw it with a crack up against Long-Tooth's head. Other Tribespeople began to hurl their greenbacks at the big cat, slowing him down enough to give the girl a moment to weigh her choices.

One way led to the tower (teetering on the edge, with Brog straining beneath it and Mog and Drog dangling from the top), where there was nothing she could do to help. The other way led to the caves and possible safety for herself.

Alone.

She ran to the tower. With the breath of the long-tooth hot on her neck. Throwing herself forward in a dive, she came sliding between Brog's legs just ahead of the cat's great head, which knocked the breath out of Brog and threw him on top of her in a heap.

The opening between the tree trunks was too narrow for the cat's body. For a moment, he stood there, spitting in rage and frustration, with the girl just beyond his reach. Then he pushed toward her, straining against the trees with all the strength of his massive shoulders. The tower lurched, the platform shifted. Mog's grip was loosening.

The girl sat where she had fallen, waiting for whatever was going to happen, only dazedly curious as to whether she would die beneath the wreck of the tower or in the jaws of the long-tooth.

Brog tried to use his club, but the space was too tight. He pushed back against the overwhelming force of the great cat. "He too strong," he gasped.

Suddenly, the girl stood up and grabbed the club out of Brog's hands. "Well, then, let *him* do the work!" she shouted

Eyes blazing, she held the club out parallel to the ground and stepped forward before Brog could stop her. Into the reach of the beast.

In the midst of a world become strange, Long-Tooth thrilled at the chance for something he knew and understood. It was time to eat. He threw his head as far back as he could under the arch of the trees and brought the fangs down in the killing stroke.

The girl swung the club up to meet them and was knocked to the ground. Brog gasped, but when the cat lifted his head, the girl scrambled away.

The club was impaled halfway up the saber fangs. The cat shook his head, but the club stayed, driven high up by his own terrible strength. He pulled back, but the club wouldn't fit between the tree trunks. He couldn't move. He had known disappointment before, he had known frustration. He had never known helplessness.

The girl sucked in the breath that had been knocked out of her and stepped close to the trembling beast. She did what she had wanted to do all that time trapped in the cave by the ocean, when she was helpless at his mercy.

She thrust out her hand.

His eyes flinched. He had never known fear.

Her hand descended. Gently, she stroked his muzzle.

It was as soft as she had imagined.

Thirty feet above, Mog's brain was reeling with the strain and pain of his loosening grip on both Drog and the platform. He thought he had finally lost his mind when he heard what the little girl whispered.

"Do you like poetry?" she asked.

Long-Tooth had no opinion on poetry, but no creature not of his own kind had ever touched him.

Since his first kill, he had always lived alone. That touch and that voice produced unbearable feelings in him.

It felt . . . good.

With a deafening roar, Long-Tooth pulled back, straining with everything in his solitary nature. The trees stopped leaning, the platform stopped tipping. For a moment, everything was in balance.

"Grab on!" called the girl. Brog caught hold of the club as the girl stepped onto it and swung herself up onto the cat's head.

The cat's frenzied pull shattered the tree trunks and carried off club and Brog and girl as the tower came crashing back onto the High Cliff. The platform smashed down where Brog had stood, while Drog landed with a thud and a groan on a pile of rubble, and Mog landed more softly on a pile of Drog.

As Brog jumped away, the cat stood trembling, the club still tight on his fangs, the girl draped over his head, her arms around his neck.

The Tribe watched in awe. The last shadow had fled from the face of the sun.

The girl twisted to get close to the cat's ear.

241

"There once was an old long-toothed
cat," she whispered.
Who wore a strange girl like a hat,
He thought he could squeeze
In between two big trees,
But the cat was too fat, and that's that."

Long-Tooth had no comment.

She slipped down from his shoulder and stood before him. He silently lowered his head to her. They looked into each other's eyes and saw themselves reflected there.

As gently as possible, she began to hammer the club down the gleaming curve of his fangs.

Pog moved to stop her, but Brog held her back in an embrace. He had a great respect for poetry, even when it wasn't as good as his own.

The club popped off.

The cat stretched his jaws, shook his head, and looked at the girl standing there. His cold yellow eyes regained their glow.

Thrusting his fangs close to the girl, he opened his terrible mouth and almost took all the skin off her face with a big lick of his raspy cat tongue.

Long-Tooth turned, his tawny coat flashing for a moment in the brilliance of renewed sunlight. Then he was gone, bounding down the path to rejoin the aloneness to which he was accustomed.

The girl turned and walked to the panting heap of Drog and Mog. "Thank you . . ." Mog began, tiredly.

"She needs a name," Pog announced, tearfully, out of the blue. "Everything needs a name."

Mog nodded. "Yes, but I can't choose. She is too many things to me."

"Then me name," Brog broke in. "She tell stories me like. To me she be Teller. You call her what you want."

Mog looked at the girl. She shrugged. "It beats Dirty-Knees," she said.

"Thank you . . . Teller," he said, trying it out. Liking it.

The Tribespeople gathered around them. "You can get off him now," Shog said, gesturing to Drog's heaving bulk.

"When he catches his breath," Mog said, "he'll start talking again, and I couldn't bear that right now."

"He won't talk much once we throw him over the cliff!" Shog blustered.

Mog took a shaky step, with the girl helping him,

then sat on the edge of the shattered stone platform. "If you kill him, who will be your Mayor?"

A murmur ran through the crowd at that. "We can't have Drog for Mayor," said Quog.

"Why not?" asked Mog.

"He lied to us, he made us think he was better than us, he took all we owned and gave us nothing but stupid greenbacks in return."

"Can you do the food-dividing and planning for the snows?" Mog asked.

The people looked at each other, remembering how bad they had been at that.

"We could go back to the old ways," suggested Quog. "Before we had a food-divider."

"I don't think you can go back," said Mog, and most of the people nodded agreement.

"*You* could be Mayor!" suggested Shog. "I'd vote for you!"

"*I* wouldn't," said Mog. "There are things I'm good at, but Mayoring isn't one of them. Everyone should do what they're best at. Brog is a great hunter, Teller is a great teller, Pog is good at figuring things out—I think she was right about the shadow of the moon—" Pog beamed with pleasure as all agreed she had been absolutely right, although it made no sense to any of them. "And Drog is the best for Mayor."

"But he's lazy," said Quog.

"And deceitful," said Shog.

"And greedy," said Trog.

Mog laughed at them. "He was all that when you voted for him. Whose fault is it that he was true to what you knew him to be?"

They all looked sheepish at that, but Quog spoke up with "He fooled us with the big words."

"Ah," said Mog, "so it was my fault." He silenced their protests. "In a way, it was. Mouth noises are more powerful than I thought when I started making them. They can bring us together or tear us apart; they can make us understand each other or hide our deepest truths; they can bring us more than we ever had before or trick away what little we have. But once we *know* they can do all these things, whose fault is it if we let them get away with it?"

He looked back at the sprawled bulk of the once and future Mayor. "Drog is the worst of us, but he has his uses. As long as we remember what he is and expect him to try his worst, it can only be our fault if he succeeds."

Everyone thought about that for a while. Quog broke the silence. "But if Drog is still Mayor . . ." He looked around at the wreckage, the shattered trees, broken stones . . . and heaps of greenbacks. The others looked, too. Suddenly they all rushed to scoop up as many greenbacks as they could.

"Stop!" yelled Mog. "No more greenbacks!" The people hesitated, but didn't drop anything. "They're big and unwieldy, and Drog still has more than anyone. If you have to have something for exchange, pick out something small and easy to deal with."

"Like what?" asked Shog, not yet letting any of his greenbacks fall.

"Like . . . interesting leaves or . . . pinecones!" There was a lot of grumbling at that.

"Or this!" Teller suddenly burst out, rummaging through her furs.

"What is it?" asked Quog.

"You'll have to ask him," Teller replied, holding it out to Mog. "What is it?"

He looked at it and thought about it carefully. "It's gold," he said.

She held it up. It glistened in the light, like its own bit of sunshine. "Gold," the people whispered, and the thump of dropping greenbacks was heard in the land.

"There's plenty of it lying around down by the sea," she said. "I can show you where to find it."

"Gold!" they shouted. "We vote for gold! Down with greenbacks, up with gold!"

"Well done!" Mog whispered to her. "It's nothing but a rock. They can all have as much as they want, and they'll never try to wear it on their heads or their hands or their ears. They'll never be crazy for gold the way they were for greenbacks."

"May I see that for a moment?" Drog asked. He was sitting up and holding out a hand. Teller hesitated, but Mog took the chunk and passed it over. "It's soft," Drog said, pushing his thumbnail into the metal.

Mog nodded. "You're thinking it's even useless for tools or weapons."

Drog was actually thinking he could shape it into little round pieces and carve an outline of his own face onto it. But he said nothing. He could be silent until the right moment came. And when the right moment came, he would know it.

Like an old long-toothed cat, he could wait.

"Let's go!" shouted the people. "Let's go for the gold!"

"Not just yet," said Mog, calling them all back together. "I have one more thing to show you."

"More words?" asked Quog.

"In a way," Mog answered.

Quog shook his head. "I don't think I can stand any more words." There were a lot of nods at that.

"You'll like this," said Mog, crouching down to grab a splinter of wood and clear a place in the dirt. "Drog gave me the idea," he said. This did not raise anyone's hopes particularly.

"He showed me what the tower looked like from one side." Mog drew in the dirt. "Two trees leaning together with the platform on the top. I imagined that first tower when he spoke the word and wrote that symbol; and that symbol made me think of the tower even when I was alone and nobody spoke the word."

"I think it would be stronger," put in Pog, "if the platform were in the middle of the trees instead of on top." She wiped out the stroke across the top, drew it in again lower.

"That's good," said Mog. "I like it. So this symbol can stand for 'tower' or 'first' or anything else I choose. And if I create more symbols—"

"Symbols for words!" said Teller, leaning down to look. "I can keep stories that way."

Pog leaned close, too. "I can put down things we need to remember."

Brog leaned in cautiously to see what Mog was drawing. "How many these things?"

"Not many," Mog said. "Not *too* many. Well, a few. As soon as you learn them, you're going to love it. Start with these."

He leaned back and gestured proudly at his scratchings on the ground:

A B C

Brog used all his new-found poetic skills to express the feelings welling up in the hearts of the Tribes-people.

"Aarrgh!" he said.